Dangerously in Love

Episode 2: Marco Silver

By Derek Da' Vinci Chatman

A.NOM.A.L.Y PUBLISHING HOUSE

ISBN-13: 978-0-578-44538-0

DEDICATION

This is book is dedicated to all of the fans of episode 1. It was you that motivated me to jump into episode 2 of this series as soon as I published episode 1. It was your calls, posts and texts, telling me how hooked you are on Nia's story, that pushed me to write late into the night on many occasions to get the story done. I would also like to thank Nia. You originally started as a concept in my mind, but it was you that wrote through me. Thank you for the story and the inspiration.

There is a little bit of Nia in all of us.

CHAPTERS

"THE MOST DANGEROUS AND MOST POWERFUL THING IN THIS WORLD, IS LOVE."

Derek Da'Vinci Chatman

CHAPTER 1: YES, WOULD HAVE BEEN EASIER

NIA, WHAT IN THE WORLD DID YOU JUST DO!!?

I'm sitting in the passenger side of Terence's car and I'm staring out the window into the abyss of nothingness as we drive up Georgia 400. Lightning bolts dart across the night sky sending cold chills up my spine. An unseasonably cold rain drenches our car. Inside the car is nothing but silence. The occasional swish of the windshield wiper breaks the monotony. This was supposed to be a special night. The night I say yes to my future. The night I say yes to the man who is going to make me his wife. Why in the world did I tell Terence no? *Why Nia? Why?*

I know the answer. It's simple….Marco, that's why. I put a halt on my future for a man who was supposed to be dead.

Terence deserves better than this. He was down on one knee, ring in hand in front of a large crowd. It was the moment every woman waits for. So what did I do? I looked Terence right in those big brown eyes and I told him no. *Damn Nia!* The look of hurt on Terence's face will be forever burned into my brain.

I should have saved Terence the pain and took an Uber right back to my mother's house. Instead, I am riding back home with my jilted lover.

Terence's shaky voice broke the silence. His voice quivered when he spoke. "Nia, I don't understand. Why won't you marry me?" I thought we were doing better."

"We were. I mean… we are. Tee, I'm so sorry." That was all I could say. How do you tell the man you love that you're secretly in love with another man who was supposed to be dead?

"I know I deserve this! Nia, I'm sorry for the way I treated you!" Terence's voice trembled.

"Babe, it's not you. It's me." I replied. It sounded like a cliché but it was true. It wasn't him. It was me and this stupid fantasy.

"So, why won't you marry me?"
I turned and looked at Terence for the first time since I got in the car. His eyes were bloodshot and filled with tears. I wish I could rewind time and go back to the moment Terence was down on one knee. I would tell him yes this time, just to spare him the pain.....who am I kidding? I know my heart wouldn't let me. Now that Marco's alive, everything has changed.

"Nia, I know I said some stupid shit to you on the day of your crash. That's my karma. I fucked this up! If I could, I would take it all back. I know I don't deserve you."

"You do deserve me. Terence, you're a good man. I just can't.."
I turned my head and focused all of my attention out of the passenger side window. It was all I could do to stop myself from crying. *Why didn't I say yes?*

CHAPTER 2: I DON'T KNOW HOW TO STOP LOVING YOU

When we arrived home, I bolted out of the car and ran right to the guest bedroom. There was no way I could share a bed with Terence. I locked the guest bedroom door, then I let my body drop on the bed. My emotions were an absolute wreck. I let it all go as my face sunk into my pillow. *How in the world was Marco alive?* This didn't make any kind of sense. *Was I seeing things?* I couldn't have. Harley saw the same thing I saw. Marco was alive! I rolled over on my back and grabbed the remote control from the night stand. I sat up, pointed it at the T.V and took pleasure in seeing my haggard reflection in the black screen disappear. I scoured the T.V menu in search of CNN. Lord knows, the last time I watched this channel. The story of the freed hostages was the breaking news story. CNN was able to partially identify the three hostages, two were news reporters and the third was an unknown soldier.

"It's Marco Silver! You idiots!" I screamed at the TV screen. I was obsessed. I would spend the rest of the night waiting for CNN to confirm the identity of the unknown soldier. In my heart of hearts I knew it was Marco, but I had to hear the words come out of the news anchor's mouth. "The unknown soldier has been identified. It's Marco Silver."

After gazing at the T.V. for a few hours, I had a sudden urge to pee. My bladder was about to explode. I looked down at the clock on my cell phone. It's freakin' 4 am and I had missed quite a few calls, three calls from Harley and three from Terence. I was so caught up in the news I didn't even realize my phone rang.

I opened the door to the guest room slowly. It was late and I was praying Terence was asleep in the bedroom. I couldn't look at him in the face right now, the guilt would be too much. As I crept out of the guest bedroom door, I could see Terence lying on the floor right next to the door. My heart sunk. *Poor guy.* He had a pillow, a blanket and a half empty bottle of Jack Daniels beside him. He must have been waiting for me to come out. I looked down at him. He looked heartbroken. *I'm so sorry, Terence!* Terence hadn't given up on me, just like he promised.

I tiptoed past him slowly, trying my hardest not to wake him up. I rushed into the bathroom as fast as I could. I didn't turn on the lights for fear of waking Terence. I did my business then I rushed back to the guest bedroom. As I exited the bathroom, I could see a large shadow on the wall near the guest bedroom. *Damnit!* Terence was standing at the entrance of the guest bedroom door. He took a big swig from the bottle of Jack before speaking.

"Nia, I don't understand why you don't want to be my wife. I'm a good guy... Damnit Nia, I love you!" Terence was drunk but sincere. I wish I could just tell him the truth, but the truth made no sense.

"Terence go to bed. You're drunk!"
"You don't love me anymore. Do you?" Terence looked desperate. I hugged him and gave him a kiss on the cheek. The kiss probably made the situation worse, but it felt right in the moment.

"Nia, I don't know how to stop loving you. You're my world. You make me who I am. I want you to be my......wife." Terence said right before passing out on his feet. *Oh no, Terence!* I rushed to catch him before he fell to the floor. Terence slumped on my shoulder as I struggled to walk him to the master bedroom. He kept mumbling how much he loved me between his vomit infused burps. After lying him down on the bed, Terence looked up at me and smiled.

"I don't know what I would do without you, Nia."

Terence looked like a drunken angel who just had his wings clipped.

I am so confused. What do I do? It was like Marco and Terence were playing tug of war with my emotions.

I walked back into the guest room and turned off the TV and got into bed. I didn't lock the guest bedroom door this time. I don't know if I did it on accident or if I did it on some subconscious level. Regardless of my motives, I was happy when Terence crept into the room twenty minutes later and got into bed with me. He hugged me from behind. His body felt good against mine. *Ahhhh!* I'm not going to lie….I needed it. He held me tight until I fell asleep in his arms. *I'm so confused!*

The next morning I awoke and snuck out of bed. Terence was still fast asleep. The bottle of Jack Daniels lay empty on the nightstand by the side of the bed. I tiptoed into the living room and turned the TV to CNN. I put the volume on low so I wouldn't wake Terence. I was so obsessed. I had to see if they identified Marco. I watched as Anderson Cooper confirmed they had more breaking news on the identity of the unknown soldier.

"In a shocking turn of events. CNN has been able to confirm the identity of the unknown soldier who was held hostage with two news reporters by the MAIO terrorist group. The soldier has been identified as Marco Silver.

Marco Silver, a decorated Marine, served the United States armed forces for over twenty years and according to our sources was killed in an apparent car accident on U.S soil earlier this year. This discovery unveils even more questions about the identity and story of our mystery man, Marco Silver.

Mr. Silver is being flown back to his hometown, Atlanta to be reunited with his wife, Sarah. I can only imagine the excitement his wife must feel. Her husband presumed dead, has now been confirmed alive. We will keep you posted as more information develops in this bizarre twist of events."

I took a deep breath! CNN just confirmed Marco was alive!!! And he was being flown back here to Atlanta!! I had to see Marco. I know he doesn't have a clue who I am, but I have to meet him. Thoughts began to race through my head. If that wasn't Marco in the car accident, than who was it? And whose lungs do I have in my body?

As Terence slept, I packed a few things in a duffle bag and headed over to my mother's house. Me being there was torture enough. I decided to stay with my mom for a few days until I got my mind in the right place.

I got in my car and drove off. I turned off the radio so it wouldn't be a distraction. I needed time to think and take in all that happened. In a 24 hour period, my entire life had been turned upside down, again. *I can't believe Marco is alive and headed home!* Within the year, I have gone through some dramatic life altering events. *Is life trying to tell me something? Is the universe trying to tell me I was heading down the wrong path?* I don't know exactly where I'm headed, but I'm going to let my heart lead me. I don't care what anyone else thinks.

As I drove up to my mother's house, I noticed two cars parked in the driveway. I recognized one of the cars, Cliff's white Nissan Maxima and the other I had never seen before. It was a nice Mercedes, but a tad bit thugged' out, with big oversized chrome wheels and dark tinted windows. *What is Cliff doing at mom's house? He should be at work right now.* I thought to myself.

I parked my car on the street and walked up the driveway. I decided to knock on the front door, ignoring the key I had in my purse. If my mother had a guest, I didn't want to surprise them by just walking in.

As I waited for the door to open, I could hear a heated argument going on inside. I knocked again. This time harder.

"What the hell is going on?" I said aloud.

Curiosity was getting the best of me. I couldn't wait any longer. I started to rifle through my purse for my keys when the front door suddenly opened. It was my mother. Her eyes looked bloodshot, like she had been crying.

"What's the matter, momma?"

My mom looked frantic. I had never seen her like this.

"It's Abony. She's in the kitchen." My mother said while pointing towards the back of the house. Without hesitation, I brushed past my mom and rushed into the house. I had to find out what was wrong with my little sister. It had to be serious if it brought my mother to tears.

As I rushed through the living room, I was surprised by my nephew, Andy. He was sitting on the living room couch staring blankly at the T.V.

mounted on the wall. The courts must've given Abony custody of Andy for a few days. Her last drug test must have come back clean.

As I approached the kitchen, I could hear two men yelling. One of the voices I recognized as Cliff's and the other sounded vaguely familiar, but I couldn't quite place it. I was just about to walk into the kitchen when Andy got up from the couch and stood in front of me. I looked down at little Andy and his awkward appearance. He was wearing what he always wore; a red hoody, black shorts, Nike slides and an Iron Man mask. It didn't matter if it was winter, spring or fall, Andy always wore the same outfit. It was his favorite.

Andy removed the Iron Man mask from his face and placed in on top of his head. His eyes were droopy and sad and his face gaunt. It looked like he hadn't eaten in days.

"My mommies hurt auntie!" Andy said to me.

"What's the matter, baby?" I questioned.

"Mommies boyfriend hit her. I tried to stop him auntie. I did. I really did… but he hit me too!"

WHAT THE FUCK!!! The news hit me like a ton of bricks. I was going to fucking kill that fucking Swag ass asshole if he laid a hand on my family! My poor nephew had to witness this shit too!

I gathered my composure for the sake of my nephew. He had already seen too much anger and violence in his life. I didn't want to add to the trauma. "Aunties baby, everything is going to be alright. I'm going to help your mommy." I picked up Andy and gave him a giant hug. Andy hugged me back, tightly. His body was so frail. I put Andy down and he ran back to the couch and his Iron man cartoon.

I walked into the kitchen, Abony was sitting at the kitchen table with a bag of frozen broccoli held tightly against her left eye. Cliff was standing above her. He was in a heated conversation with someone else in the room. It had to be the person driving the Benz.

"I DON'T GIVE A SHIT WHO HE IS. I'M GOING DOWN THERE AND I'M GOING TO BEAT HIS ASS!" Cliff yelled.

"Calm down, son. I will handle this!" The man barked back. I finally recognized the voice. It was the man I hadn't seen since I was three years old. It was the man (if that's what you want to call him) I spent my entire childhood writing letters to, begging him to come home, begging to come to my soccer games, my birthday parties and Christmas. Cliff was arguing with my sperm donor of a father.

"WHAT'S GOING ON IN HERE?" I asked commandingly. Surprised by my voice, Cliff and my sperm donor looked over at me. It was kind of scary how much they looked alike. They both had the same body shape, broad shoulders and peanut shaped head.

"It's Abony! That piece of shit boyfriend of hers decided to use her as his punching bag." Cliff said. I had never seen my brother so upset.

"Cliff, calm down. It was my fault. I shouldn't have walked in on Swag when he's working." Abony said softly.

I could see the anger rising in my sperm donor's face. It actually looked like he gave a half a damn about my sister.

"Baby girl, it's never your fault. A man should NEVER under any circumstance, put his hand on a woman!" Our sperm donor responded. I had no idea this man knew what it meant to treat a woman properly. I stared at our sperm donor. He was old and wrinkled. He had turned into that guy who dressed hip and didn't realize he was too old and way past his prime. He had on baggie skinny jeans, a baseball cap and a neck and mouth full of gold.

"Pops, we can't let that punk get away with this." Cliff explained. "I know son, but we have to handle it the way the streets handle it. I got hitters on my team. We will scoop that plug wanna' be up and take care of him!"

Abony stood up and begged Cliff and our sperm donor to leave Swag alone. They ignored her. Swag had set the wheels in motion and there is nothing Abony could do to stop my sperm donor and Cliff now.

"Swag loves me, please don't hurt him!" Abony pleaded. Abony was right to be afraid for Swag's life. Our donor literally owned the streets. He was one of the biggest and ruthless drug dealers in the city. I'm not proud of it, but the Wright name carries a legacy in the streets. I looked over at my beaten and bruised sister. There is nothing worse in my book, than a woman who defends a man who beats her. I couldn't hold my tongue. I guess it's the mini psychologist in me.

"Abony, why are you putting up with this shit?" "Nia.. I know… I know, but Swag didn't mean it. It was my fault"

"It's not your fault! Swag is a piece of shit, and he's not going to stop until he kills you!"

"Oh, bruh' not gonna' put his hands on her again!" Our donor chimed in.

"Dad, please don't!" Abony pleaded. Our sperm donor grabbed Abony. I could see his finger gripping her shoulders tightly as he shook her back and forth.

"What's the matter with you girl? I won't kill him. He just won't have a hand to put on you again." I jumped in between our sperm donor and Abony, removing his hand from her shoulders.

"You are just like him!" I yelled at our sperm donor.

"Just like who?"

"You are just like that fucking SWAG!" Our donor looked at me like I had two heads.

"What do you mean? I aint' like that wanna' be mother fucka'! I own these streets! He's a fake ass thug, selling weed from his apartment. All I need to do is give the order and bruh' will be excommunicated. If you know what I mean?"

I could tell I touched a nerve, but it was true and I let our sperm donor know it. Abony dates assholes like Swag because our sperm donor is an asshole like Swag. Our sperm donor slammed his fist down on the counter and began to approach me. He had anger in his eyes. I couldn't tell if he was going to hug me or strangle me. Cliff jumped in front of our donor before I could find out his intentions.

"I don't have to take this crap!" Our donor yelled as Cliff tried to restrain him.

"I aint' gotta' take this shit from you, Nia! I'm out of here!" Cliff loosened his grip as our donor made his way out of the kitchen.

"Do what you do best! Walk out on your responsibilities." I yelled back at our donor. I could see anger with a hint of guilt take over his face.

"Don't worry, baby girl. I got this." Our sperm donor said to Abony as he walked out. Abony made one last attempt to plead with our donor. He had murder in his eyes as he brushed Abony aside. The truth hurts and

I'm glad I said it. He can't just walk in and out of our lives whenever he pleases. We made it this far without him. We don't need him now.

I could hear the sound of screeching tires as our donor sped out of my mother's driveway. I looked over to Abony, she looked beaten both physically and mentally. Gone were her "hoochie mama" clothes and all of her makeup. She was in a simple pair of jeans and sneakers with her hair swept back in a bun. She looked like the sweet Abony of old. She was beautiful, despite the black and blue bruise under her eye.

"Why did you call him?" I said to my mother as she walked into the kitchen.

"He's your father. I didn't know who else to call." My mother said unapologetically. I knew my mom meant well but I wish she would have just called me instead. I walked over to Abony and gave her a hug. I fought back my judgments. She had been through a lot in her life and the last thing she needed now were my "I told you so's."

I convinced Cliff to let the drama go for now and return to work. It was a hard thing for him to do. He had taken over the fatherly duties in our family and felt it was his job to protect Abony. We all knew what was best for her. All we had to do now was convince her to leave Swag and her crazy life.

My mom and I didn't really have to utter a word as we sat at the kitchen table with Abony. Abony did all of the talking. She talked about getting her life back on track, she talked about getting full custody of Andy.

"This life is not just mine, it's Andy's too. I have to do what's right for him. I can't have my son around Swag and all his crap."

Abony was finally seeing the light. Sometimes it takes hitting rock bottom for us to see clearly.

After our conversation, I went to the car and grabbed my duffle bag. My mom watched me from the kitchen window as I returned to the house with my bag in hand. I didn't have to utter a word, no need for an explanation. My mom just smiled and watched me walk into my old bedroom. I put my duffle bag on the bed and turned the old TV in my bedroom to CNN. I sat down on the bed and watched intently as I hoped to get more information on Marco and his return home.

CHAPTER 3: KILLER FOR HIRE

I flipped back and forth through every news channel hoping to see a news report or any info on Marco. It was so freaking frustrating. Every news program was filled with the typical nonsense. I could give two craps about who shot who last night or who robbed what bank or what place was bombed yesterday. That's why I never watch the news. It's always filled with horrible depressing stories.

After searching through what seemed like every channel on the cable lineup, I finally found a local news station doing a report on Marco's return home. I watched intently as the news reporter stood on the Tarmac in front of a small jet, mobbed by other reporters who were waiting to get the first pictures of Marco's return home.

I have to admit, I was a little jealous, when pictures of Marco and Sarah's wedding flashed on the TV screen. *Sarah could care less about Marco!* Marco should be returning home to me, not her. Where was she anyway? If it were me and my dead husband was returning home, I would be waiting at the airport for my man with open arms. She was probably off somewhere getting freaky with Todd one last time.

I watched intently as the camera zoomed on Marco as he walked down the airplane stairs. *Poor Marco!* He looked beaten and confused, like the life had been sucked out of him. I wish I could be there to comfort him. I would hug him for hours and tell him everything was going to be alright. I caught a glimpse of Sarge standing at the bottom of the airplanes stairs. *Thank goodness, Marco was going to finally see a familiar face!* Marco had been through a lot of trauma. I could only imagine what he was feeling. Sarge hugged his old friend and Marco smiled for the first time. I smiled too, Marco was finally home safe and sound. Sarge walked Marco to the back of his limo. I watched intently as the camera flashes illuminated Marco's face. It was a little bittersweet as the news reporter reminded me and the rest of the world that Marco was about to be reunited with his wife, Sarah. Sarah had no idea how lucky she was.

O.K, now that Marco is home and safe, I should go see him, right? I have no idea what I would say or do, all I know is I have to look into the eyes of the man I fell in love with, the man who wrote those beautiful love letters, the man who donated his lungs to me. I had to share the air with the man I thought I would never meet, a man I believed to be dead. I couldn't do it alone though, I didn't have the courage. So I called the only person on the face of the earth who knew what I was going through.

Harley didn't hesitate when she received my call, she left the office immediately and came by and picked me up. She looked like a giddy little school girl when she arrived in my mother's driveway.

"Are you nervous? What are you going to say when you see him? What are you going to say to Sarah?" Harley's questions were coming a mile a minute. She was so excited. Hell, I was excited too. I was about to see Marco!

Harley put the top down on her BMW and put her foot on the gas and we were in Marco and Sarah's neighborhood in a matter of minutes. When we arrived at the security gate, the Security Guard refused us access. He told us he could only allow access tenants or people on the approved visitors list. The list was rather large considering Marco's return home. I told Harley to back up the car. *We tried, right?* Plus the "chicken" in me was ok with retreating. I had no idea what I would say to Marco, anyway. I looked over at Harley, she had a devious look on her face. My girl was up to something.

"Don't worry, I got this." Harley said as she gave me a wink. Harley unbuttoned the top button of her blouse, revealing a little cleavage. Harley didn't have much up there, but my girl knew how to work it. I watched as Harley leaned in and smiled at the Security Guard. He smiled back. The balding, average looking guy had never dealt with a beautiful vixen like Harley. *He didn't stand a chance.* I smiled and wondered how many times Harley used this trick to get her into places. Harley fumbled through her purse and found a scrap piece of paper. Harley scribbled a fake telephone number on the scrap paper and handed it to the security guard.

"Is this your number?" The security guard said with a cracked voice. "Well of course. What's your name?" Harley said in her best Marylyn Monroe impression.

"It's… Ro… Rodrick." The guard stuttered.

"Well Rodrick, are you sure we're not on the list?" Rodrick took a deep breath and a giant gulp as his eyes darted back and forth between Harley's supermodel face and her protruding breasts. Rodrick looked like he just climaxed as sweat dripped down his brow. Despite not being on the list, Rodrick the security guard opened the security gate and let us in. I smiled as Harley cruised through the gate. I looked in the rearview mirror and could see the guard staring down at Harley's fake phone number. *Poor Rodrick.*

We drove slowly through the community of houses. We didn't have a hard time finding Marco and Sarah's house because it was mobbed by reporters. There were news vans and reporters from every major news network. The reports covered Marco and Sarah's lawn as they waited to catch a glimpse of Marco. Harley parked the car a few houses down from Marco and Sarah's house. We tried our best to get close to the house, but we couldn't because there was a police barricade surrounding it.

I felt butterflies dancing all through my stomach. "Harley please take me home. I can't do this! Let's come back another day." I pleaded.

"Oh no, I got this, girl." Harley wasn't having it. "I can get us past that silly barricade."

I had no doubt in my mind, especially after seeing Rodrick the security guard crumple under Harley's powers. I could only imagine what other tricks she had up her sleeve.

We walked up to the Police barricade. There were two big officers standing in front of the yellow wooden barricade. Harley did her runway model strut up to the barricade. I walked behind her trying my best to hold in my laugh. The two officers zoned right in on Harley, just as she planned.

"Sorry ma'am, only members of the press are allowed access." The burley officer with the thick neck remarked. Harley walked right up to the officer and stood nose to nose with him. The officers cheeks turned bright red. *It was working.*

"Officer, can you help us please? My friend is Marco's sister and she hasn't seen him in years." Harley said in a sexy voice as she pointed her finger in my direction. The officer looked over at me. He looked flustered. I am sure he has dealt with all types of crimes and criminals, but the police academy never taught him about how to deal with a five foot ten inch blonde in stilettos. Before he could respond, the officers partner stepped in between Harley and the flustered officer.

"Excuse me ma'am, I am going to need you to back up." The officer said while placing his hand on Harley's shoulder. Harley turned around and smiled at me right before she went into her tirade. I guess if the beauty doesn't work then go with the next best option.

"Listen, my girl wants to see her family! She has every right to see them!" Harley yelled in the officers ear.

"Ma'am, I don't give a crap who she is related to. Our orders are to not let anyone past the barricade." The officer yelled back.
Harley got in the officers face again. I tried to pull her back, but Harley was not having it. Harley was lucky. If this was the hood, she would have been sprawled all over the concrete. Harley started yelling at the officer even louder demanding him to let me in. Harley was causing a scene and her mini tirade was starting to draw the attention of the news reporters.

A short stubby man in a tight short sleeved shirt and black silk tie, too small for his pop belly, appeared out of the crowd of reporters.

"Gentleman, is there a problem here?" The chubby man asked.
I immediately recognized his voice. It was the detective who interviewed Terence and I after the stabbing at the hospital.

"This lady says they are related to the Silvers and they want to get in." The officer looked relieved. The detective had come to his rescue.

"Sorry young lady, if your friend is truly related to the Silvers then she can come back later and visit them. As of right now, no one is allowed past these barricades." The detective said to Harley. I stepped in front of Harley. I had to talk to this detective. I found it kind of odd that a homicide detective would be at a press event. *Shouldn't he be out trying to solve a murder or something?*

You should have seen the look on detective Arpin's face when I appeared from behind Harley's back.

"Nia....Nia, Wright? What are you doing here?"
I was glad the detective remembered me. Now I could demand some answers about the freckled man who tried to kill me.

"Have you guys been able to identify the man who tried to kill me?" Detective Arpin eyes opened wide. It was written all over his face. The detective wanted me to keep my mouth shut about the freckled killer.

"Nia, can we talk alone?" Detective Arpin requested. He wrapped his arm around my shoulder and escorted me away from earshot of Harley and the officers.

"Listen Nia, I need you to do me a big favor."
What kind of favor could the detective need from me? I thought to myself.

"I want you to forget about the guy who tried to kill you."
"Forget about him? What are you talking about? The guy killed a nurse and tried to kill me and my fiancé! You want me to just forget about him?" The detective must be insane. Why would he want me to forget about the killer? Detective Arpin stepped in close and started to whisper.

"Yes, forget about him? I am telling you this for your own safety. Don't ever mention his name again."

"So what about his murder trial? Am I supposed to just forget about that too?" Detective Arpin looked annoyed.

"Nia, there won't be a trial?"
"How can there not be a trial? The man killed a nurse!"

I was getting beyond frustrated and detective Arpin was starting to piss me off. I watched the detectives eyes slowly transform from confidence to fear. The detective looked around to make sure no one could hear him before he spoke.

"I was told by my boss to let that fucking murderer go. He couldn't tell me why, but he told me that someone very important wanted him free. I was told to get rid of any evidence of this man's existence. Nia, this man is connected. I don't know to who, but he is connected. I don't think his attempt to kill you was personal. I think he was hired to kill you. That's why I am telling you to let this go. I received an anonymous tip that Marco may be in danger and that's why I'm here. I have questions about this killer too, but I can't officially investigate him."

The detectives words left me in shock. Who in the world would want this killer to be free? Why was he trying to kill me? My mind began to race as fear took over all of my emotions. That's why he was peeping in Sarah's windows. He was probably hired to kill her too!

All types of thoughts raced through my head. The car accident that put me in a coma for six months and supposedly killed Marco was not an accident at all. I bet the freckled killer was hired to kill Marco, too.

CHAPTER 4: MARCO SILVER

It took an entire week for the news story to die down. The story of Marco and the returned hostages was now yesterday's news. The headlines were quickly replaced by rapper turned music mogul, T-Drillz, secret marriage to Pop princess Taylor Eubanks, the daughter of Presidential candidate Thomas Eubanks. FOX News did an entire segment on the unlikely couple and how T-Drillz's rapper status is scaring off Thomas Eubanks conservative supporters. This came on right before the segment on Marco Silver and the conspiracy theory around his faked death. FOX news did an entire exposé on how the coroner and dental records of the man killed in the car accident were a DNA match to Marco. The panelists on the show theorized a government cover up, but couldn't prove it. Despite all of their investigations, they could not identify the body of the man lying in Georgia National Cemetery with Marco Silver's name on his tombstone.

I had my hand on my chest as I watched the news on Marco. The entire time I kept wondering whose lungs I had in my body and why in the world would they fake Marco's death? My mind was racing. I had to get answers. So I decided to drive by Marco's neighborhood. This had become my nightly ritual. Each night the amount of reporters camped out in front of Marco's home slowly dwindled. They were probably camped out at T-Drillz's house now.

As I drove by the entrance gate, Rodrick the security guard nodded his head, smiled and let me right through. He doesn't even question why I'm in the neighborhood anymore and that's all thanks to Harley. Turns out, she accidentally gave Rodrick her real telephone number. Harley was shocked when Rodrick called her the first time. My girl Harley hung up on him at first and then she eventually called Rodrick back. Can you believe they talk every night now and have plans to go on an actual date? Harley may have finally found her man.

I turned the headlights off as I drove by Marco and Sarah's home. I kinda' felt like a creep, but what is a girl to do when she's in stalker mode? As I approached the house, I was hit with a little dose of reality blended with a whole lotta' fear. *What if Marco hates me? What if he turned out to be a jerk or something like that?* Crazy thoughts ran through my head. I knew it all boiled down to my nerves. I felt like a sixteen year old girl afraid to approach her crush.

I gathered my nerve and eased my car behind a red Fiat parked across the street from Marco and Sarah's house. The Fiat looked out of place for some odd reason. I paid it no never mind. I had more important things to think about. "Nia, it's now or never!" I whispered under my breath as I got out of the car and walked up the driveway to the front door. As I approached, I noticed a beautiful pot of sunflowers resting on the ground by the side of the porch. They reminded me of Marco and his meadow of sunflowers. I focused my thoughts on the flowers. "Nia, you got this." I said to myself right before ringing the doorbell.

Sarah greeted me at the front door. Well, I don't know if "greeted" would be the appropriate word. We both stared at each other awkwardly. All I could picture was her dressed in that god awful leather maids outfit with the matching mask and whip in her hands.

"What the hell are you doing here?" Sarah asked rudely.

No she didn't! "Excuse me.......?" My blood went to full boil. *Sarah don't know who she's messing with!* I took a deep breath and counted to three before finishing my sentence. I had to keep my cool.

"I'm here to see Marco."

"Marco?" Sarah replied.

"Yeah Marco, the guy who donated his lungs to me. You know, you're husband, the man your skank ass is fucking cheating on!!" I could see the vein on the side of Sarah's neck begin to pulsate. *O.k., so I did a horrible job with keeping my composure. Don't judge. It's not like I wasn't telling the truth.*

"How dare you come up here looking for my husband and then accuse me of cheating on him?!!"

"Oh don't front, Sarah! I saw you and you saw me!"
"You mean that day I caught you peeping outside of my bedroom window? What where you doing there anyway?" Sarah questioned.

"I wasn't peeping. I was…." *Ok, she's right. I was peeping in her window, but that wasn't me playing peeping Tom. It was the freckled killer peeping in her damn windows.*

"Regardless of how I got there. You know what I saw… I saw you in your little freak show outfit spanking that little personal trainer of yours!" You should have seen the look on Sarah's face. She turned beet red. It looked like hot steam was going to come spraying out of her nostrils. I think steroid queen had enough of me. I don't care how much this chick can squat, she did not want to mess with me. Sarah placed her thick muscular index finger in front of her lips in attempt to shush me.

"Shhhhh….All this noise is going to get Marco upset."
Now she's going to play stupid? I know her game. I was not going to

keep quiet. Marco needed to know the truth of what was going on while he was away defending our country. I scanned the room behind her. Sarah stood in front of the doorway. She was purposely blocking my view.

"MARCO!" I yelled into the open living room. There was nothing but silence. Silly me, I guess I kind of expected Marco to trot into the living room on the back of a black stallion while wearing a knights outfit. *A girl can dream, right?* All I want to do was see him, breathe the same air he breathes and see his smile in person. Plus, he had to know the truth about Sarah.

I could hear a conversation going on in the kitchen. It sounded like two men laughing and joking but I couldn't see beyond Sarah's massive body. I yelled Marco's name again. "MARCO!"

"What the hell do you think you're doing? Get off my porch!" Sarah yelled. She was about the slam the door in my face when whoever was in the kitchen interrupted her.

"Sarah, is everything ok here?" Todd said from behind Sarah.

My heart suddenly fell down to my knees. My head began to throb as the room began to spin. I felt like I was going to pass out or throw up on my shoes. It was not because of Todd and his stupid spandex. It was the man standing next to Todd that made me feel like this. It was the man I see in my nightmares. The man Detective Arpin told me to forget about. The man I saw kill a nurse. The man who stabbed Terence. The freckled killer was standing in Marco's living room, sharing a drink with Marco's wife's lover.

"And, who is this?" The freckled killer said with a devilish smile. He extended his hand and I refused to shake it. It was not out of anger but out of fear.

"This is Nia, and she was just leaving." Sarah said.

"Oh, that's a shame….Nia, is such a beautiful woman. It would be rude not to offer her a drink." The freckled killer said coyly. He was playing with my emotions. Why would he pretend to be friendly with me now? Then it hit me. *Where in the world is Marco!? Did the freckled killer get to him!? Was Sarah and Todd in on this too!? Oh God, Marco!*

"Where is he?....Where's, Marco?" I demanded. All three of them looked at me like I was crazy.

"Nia, calm down. Marco's not in any condition to see anyone right now." Sarah replied.

"I'm not going to calm down! I know what you guys are up to and I'm not going to let it happen!"

"Nia, you sound upset. You should probably go home. I was going to leave after this drink. I could take you home. Do you live close by?" The freckled killer said calmly and coolly.

"I am not leaving with you and I am not going to let you hurt Marco!" I shoved Sarah aside, forcing my way into the living room. *Freckled killer or no freckled killer, I was not going to let them harm Marco!*

"MARCO! MARCO!" I yelled.

"NIA STOP! Marco is not doing good right now!" Sarah demanded.

"Where is he?"

"He's in the back bedroom." I started to make my way to the back bedroom when Sarah stopped me.

"Nia, Marco's going through some type of post-traumatic stress. He doesn't even recognize me! He spends most of his time cooped up in our bedroom closet. Nia, he's frightened and delusional. All he talks about is his mother and some stupid sunflower field.

I could feel my heart drop. Poor Marco, lord only knows what they did to him while he was held hostage.

"I have to see him!"

"You're wasting your time, Nia. I tried everything. There is nothing you can do to help!" Sarah assured.

"Well maybe if you spent more time with your husband instead of getting all weird and freaky with your damn personal trainer, Marco wouldn't be cooped up in the closet!"

"I think it's time for you to leave!" Todd said angrily.
I looked at Todd like he had two heads. There was no way his little spandex ass was going to stop me from seeing Marco.

"I will leave when I'm good and ready to leave! And right now I'm not ready to leave!"

I nudged Todd out of my way and made a B-line to the bedroom. Sarah ran ahead of me and blocked the bedroom door. I walked right up to her and stood nose to nose.

"If you know what's good for you, you will get out of my way!"
I was seeing red. I'm not going to lie, Sarah's biceps were probably bigger than my leg. She could have probably crushed me in two if she wanted to. Sarah paused for a moment looking me dead in my bloodshot eyes. She wasn't about this life. Sarah stepped aside and I walked into their bedroom and over to the closet.

The room was pitch black, so I turned on all of the lights. I took a deep breath before opening the closet door. I didn't know what I expected to see, so I braced myself for the worse.

At first all I could see was a ball of blankets in the corner of the closet. I took another deep breath then I pulled back the blankets. Marco was curled up in a ball underneath them. He had a thick unkempt beard and smelled like he hadn't showered in months. Marco's whole body was shaking with chills.

"What in the world did they do to you?" I said to Marco. Marco continued to shake back and forth, oblivious to my presence.

"Momma.. I will meet you in the meadow."

"Momma.. I will meet you in the meadow."

"Momma.. I will meet you in the meadow."

"Momma.. I will meet you in the meadow."

That's all Marco would say as he stared off into space. I reached out and touched Marco's hand. I dreamed many nights of holding his hand, but I had never envisioned it like this.

"I'm sorry." I whispered in Marco's ear. I tried to hug him, but Marco shuddered and curled deeper into a ball.

"See, I told you he was bat shit crazy! All he keeps talking about is some damn meadow of sunflowers!" Sarah said from outside of the closet. Sarah had no clue about the meadow of sunflowers. Of course, I knew because I actually read Marco's love letters, unlike her dumbass. I looked around the room. Todd stood by Sarah side. The freckled killer was nowhere to be found. *Where the hell did he go?*

I had no time to worry about him. Marco needed me. I ran out of the bedroom and out to the front porch as Sarah and Todd looked on. I remembered the small garden of sunflowers at the entrance of the house.

I don't know what I was going to do with them or how they were going to help, but I knew I had to get them to Marco. I looked across the street. The red Fiat I parked behind when I arrived, was gone. *It must have belonged to the freckled killer. I probably foiled his plans.*

I hopped off the porch and plucked a few sunflowers. Then I ran back to the bedroom and over to the closet.

"What are you doing? " Sarah questioned.

I didn't answer because I didn't know either. I walked into the closet and put the sunflowers in Marco's hand, hoping they would ease his pain. Marco stopped shaking and looked down at the sunflowers. He stared at them for a moment, then put the sunflowers up to his nose. He closed his eyes and inhaled deeply. I could see what looked like a slight smile forming on the side of his lips. *They're working!* I thought to myself. Marco turned his head and looked me right in my eyes. I had dreamed of this moment and it was actually happening. I smiled back at Marco. I could feel a tear roll down my cheek. I know we made a connection. I know I broke through to Marco, even if it was for a brief second.

"Oh God, I killed her! I killed her!"

"I killed her!"

"I killed her!"

Marco slight smile turned into a frown. He was getting angry. I watched in horror as he clinched his teeth and began pounding his fists on the hardwood floor in the closet. Marco stood up in the closet and started ripping the clothes from the shelves and began throwing them out of the closet. I tried to stop him, but the Marco I fell in love with wasn't there. This was some beast or wild animal.

"MARCO, NO!!" I yelled.

Marco jumped out of the closet and ran into the bedroom. He grabbed the television off of the dresser and threw it across the room. Then he ran over to the bed and flipped the mattress upside down.

"I killed her!"

"I killed her!" He kept screaming.

Todd ran over and jumped on Marco in an attempt to stop him from destroying the room. Marco was too strong for him so Sarah jumped in as well. They both tackled Marco to the ground.

"SEE WHAT YOU DID? GET OUT OF HERE NOW BEFORE I CALL THE POLICE!" Sarah screamed as they struggled to keep control of Marco. I looked on in horror as they struggled. I felt so bad for Marco, he may be traumatized for the rest of his life. I looked into his eyes as he struggle to get free. I didn't say a word. The language I was speaking to Marco was with my eyes. I promised him I would do everything in my power to help him, no matter what it took. I took a deep breath and walked out of the room.

CHAPTER 5: I LOVE YOU

I pulled my car into the garage. I had no idea why I drove home. I know a part of it had to do with the fact that I was heartsick over Marco, plus I really couldn't deal with the drama right now at my mom's house with Abony, Swag and my sperm donor. My emotions were mixed, confused. I had an urge to see Terence. I need his comfort. I need his smile. I need someone I can talk to, someone who gets me. I feel kinda' guilty and I don't want to lead Terence on, but I just need him right now.

I closed the garage door and walked into the kitchen. I put my keys on the kitchen counter and looked in the fridge for something to eat. I wasn't really hungry. I just needed something, anything to take my mind off of Marco. Visions of Marco camped out in my mind. I kept seeing the horror in his eyes as he laid curled up in a ball in the closet. Then my mind darted to the freckled killer. *Why was he at Marco and Sarah's house?* None of this made any sense.

As I closed the fridge door I was startled by Terence. He was standing at the entrance of the kitchen. He must have heard me come into the house. I looked over at him, my eyes red and watered. Terence looked back at me and smiled. I walked over to him and buried my face into his chest. Without asking a single question about my return, Terence held me tight. I let all of my emotions go right then and there in Terence's embrace. I let it all out, Marco, Abony, my father, losing my job, the car accident, the freckled killer…everything. Terence rocked me back and forth, I could feel him absorbing my pain. He picked me up off of my feet and carried me over to the leather sofa in the living room.

He sat me down on the sofa and then kissed me gently on my forehead. Then he began rubbing my shoulders all the way up to my temple. *God, I need this right now! I knew Terence wouldn't let me down.* He had a gentle way of doing things. He moved his hands across my body like he was molding clay. No wonder he is a good surgeon, he has great hands.

"Do you want a glass of wine?" Terence asked softly. I told him yes. A glass of Moscato would hit the spot right about now. As I sat on the sofa, I gazed at all of the empty liquor bottles lining the coffee table. *Nia, you did this to him. You turned this man into an alcoholic.*

Terence returned to the living room with a tall glass of wine in his hand and a box tucked underneath his arm. *Why is he carrying a box?* I thought to myself right before my heart stopped. It only took me a second to realize he was carrying the box with Marco's love letters, ring and IPad.

I FORGOT TO MAIL THE BOX BACK TO SARAH!
I started to feel nauseous as all of my anxiety returned to my body. Terence walked over and handed me the glass of wine. I expected him to pour it over my head, instead he placed it gently in my hands. I looked in his eyes, Terence seemed unfazed. *Maybe he didn't open the box.* I prayed. That was wishful thinking. I could see the carton's seal was torn open when Terence set the box on the coffee table in front of me.

"So, is Marco the reason why you turned down my proposal?"
I was lost for words. I didn't know how to respond. I took a big sip of my wine, hoping it could buy me some time as I tried to think of a reason why I had Marco's letters.

"You don't have to say a word Nia, I know the answer."
Terence buried his face in the palms of his hands and took a deep breath.

I closed my eyes hoping I could be magically transported to another planet.

"I deserve this. It's all my fault. I am the reason why we're not married right now. If I hadn't taken you for granted you wouldn't have gotten in that damn accident."

"Terence you had nothing to do with this."

Maybe a part of it was true, but Terence wasn't the reason why I fell in love with Marco. Terence and I were not in the right place when I got in the accident. We both played a role in our breakup. We weren't ready for a marriage.

I apologized to Terence for keeping this from him. Even though I never expected Marco to return. I was still guilty of having feelings for someone else, even if the person was a ghost.

"Do you love him?" Terence asked cautiously.

I could tell he didn't really want to hear my answer.

"Terence, I thought he was dead."

"You're not answering the question. Do you love him?"

"Terence…."

"Nia, tell me the truth."

"Yes… I love him." I blurted out. My revelation felt awful. But, it was out there, finally out in the open. Terence closed his eyes. Even though he knew the answer, the news crushed him.

"Do you still love me?" Terence said as he held his hands over his heart.

"Terence, I can't answer that." I replied.

Of course I loved him. I wanted to tell him yes, but I knew if I did, it would only lead to more heartache. I couldn't let my heart go there. I was so confused. Coming here was not a good idea. *I have to get out of this house! I have to get out now!*

I got up to leave and as I made my way to the door, Terence followed me. He stood in front of the door blocking my exit.

"Nia, do you love me? Just answer the question."

"Terence don't make me answer!" I pleaded.

"It's because you do still love me. Don't you?"

"Terence, let me leave." I pleaded.

"Not until you tell me the truth! If you don't love me. then just say it! But if you have one ounce of love left for me in your heart then I can't just let you go."

I closed my eyes and thought for a moment. I fought back every urge in my body to tell Terence the truth, but I couldn't. I could feel my emotions boiling like a hot pot on a stove. Just as I was about to put my hands over my lips to hold it all in, I blurted out my answer.

"Terence, I love you!"

I could see the dimples forming in Terence's smile as my words danced in the air. A simple no would have put him out of his misery. Instead, I gave Terence a sign of hope that one day I would be his. *"Stupid, stupid, stupid, Nia." Why did I tell him that?*

Terence tried to hug me and give me a kiss. I fought back the urge, even though I desperately needed it. Terence looked at me confused as I removed his arms from around me and walked out the door. I jumped into my car and put the keys in the ignition. I had to get out of there. As I pulled off, I could see Terence in the rearview mirror. He stood inside the garage with his arms folded with a big smile on his face.

Damnit Nia, what did you do?

CHAPTER 6: NIA, YOU IN DANGER, GIRL!

I drove around the city all night until the sun came up. I had Terence and Marco on my mind the entire time. Some women can go their entire lives without finding their soul mate, lucky me, I found two. One soul mate loves me and wants to commit his life to me and the other doesn't even know I exist.

I did a lot of soul searching during my drive and I came to the conclusion that I had to make a decision. For my own sanity's sake, I had to choose who I was going to give my heart to. I couldn't go on with life, if my mind was in one place and my heart in another.

Coming to a decision wasn't easy. I had to go with what made sense. And with this, I decided to let Marco go and marry Terence. *Confusing? Yes, I know.* During my drive, all I could see was Terence's face lighting up when I told him I loved him. He was the logical choice. It made the most sense. Terence and I have history together. He loves me. *He's a smart and handsome doctor, for goodness sake!* I would be crazy to give him up! I know sista's that would stand in line for days to have a man like Terence. He was the best choice and the safest choice.

I turned the car around and headed to Marco's house. I felt like I had to at least say goodbye to the man I had never officially said hello to. Marco and I had a connection even if it was only in my mind. I had to at least make an attempt to help Marco regain some of his sanity. It was the least I could do for the man who captured my heart. I couldn't go on with life knowing Marco was suffering. I refuse to turn my back on him. I couldn't imagine marrying Terence and raising a family knowing Marco was out there lost.

I parked my car across the street from Sarah and Marco's house. I didn't really have a plan but I knew one thing for sure, I didn't want to ring the doorbell if Sarah was home. So, I sat in my car and I waited for her to leave. I knew she had to leave the house at some point. So, I waited and waited. Ten minutes turned into an hour as I dozed off to sleep in the front seat of my car.

I wasn't out long when I was awoken by the sound of a closing door. I sat up quickly, not realizing I had dozed off. I wiped the drool from my cheek as I watched Sarah walk out of her front door. She had a little pep in her step as she skipped over to Todd's house. I lowered myself in my seat, so I wouldn't be seen. After a few knocks, Todd greeted Sarah at the door.

I sat there mortified as I witnessed Todd put his tongue down Sarah's throat and his hands on her ass, as they carried their little love fest into the house. I know I'm not one to judge, but the whole thing just seemed so disrespectful. Poor Marco, he's probably cooped up in his bedroom closet while his wife is off spanking her personal trainer.

I jumped out of the car and made my way to the front door of Marco and Sarah's house. I knew I had to be swift, Lord knows how long Todd and Sarah's little freak romp would last. I tried to open the front door, but it was locked. I was about to ring the doorbell when I realized there was no way Marco was going to open the door in his condition. It left me with only one other option, the bedroom window.

I walked around to the side of the house and over to the bedroom window. The window was unlocked, so I pushed it open and made an attempt to climb inside. I couldn't really pull myself up through the window, so I grabbed a trash barrel from behind the house and used it as a step stool.

"Damn, I have to start working out again." I said to myself.

It took all my might and power to make it through the bedroom window. God blessed me with hips and a booty, but they weren't much help in getting me through that damn tiny window.

Once inside the room, I bent over and rested my hands on my knees as I struggled to catch my breath. Once I finally stopped hyperventilating, I made my way over to the bedroom closet. Just as I suspected, Marco was inside curled up into a ball under a pile of blankets.

"Marco" I called several times from the open closet door.

Marco poked his head up from under the covers and looked me right in my eyes.

"I killed her?" Marco whimpered.

"Marco, it wasn't your fault." I answered, hoping I could get through to him. Marco was reliving his past. I bet it was some sort of survival technique he used to help him survive when he was held hostage. I remember reading an article about this on Huffington Post. The article said Special Forces soldiers were trained to focus on something from their past to help them cope. This helps them keep their sanity and of course prevents them from revealing secrets if they were ever captured and tortured by the enemy. The article also mentioned the soldier going into some sort of a trance and the only way it can be broken is with a trigger the soldier set in his mind.

"I killed her. I killed her. I killed her." Marco kept repeating.

I looked at Marco's terrified face. He looked like a child, so innocent and fragile. Lord knows what those terrorists put him through.

I stepped deeper into the closet and gave Marco a hug. His body cringed when he felt my touch. I'm sure the touches he felt when he was held hostage were not as warm and friendly.

"Marco would you like to go to the meadow?"

Marco's eyes lit up.

"I have to meet my mom at her sunflower meadow. Can you take me there?"

I'm not going to lie, I wasn't comfortable with the idea of taking Marco to the meadow. What if Marco decides to go bonkers on me like he did last night? I paused and thought about it for a moment and then it hit me. What if the meadow is Marco's trigger? It made perfect sense. What did I have to lose?

"Yes, I will bring you to the meadow." I said to Marco.

I grabbed Marco by the hand and guided him out to my car. He followed me like a little boy on his way to school. As we walked out of the front door, I kept my eye on Todd's house. I had no idea what I would do if Sarah came strutting out. I just knew I had to get Marco in my car as fast as I could. I opened the passenger side door and sat Marco in the seat. As I put his seatbelt around him I caught Marco staring at me. Our eyes met and Marco smiled. It was a real smile, like his eyes were thanking me for helping him. I smiled back and then I buckled him up.

The car ride to Marco's parents farm was quiet. Marco slept while I occasionally glanced over at the man I once believed to be a ghost. It still seemed so surreal. Marco was actually alive and sitting in my car. I couldn't have imagined this in my wildest dreams and let me tell you

Marco was in some of my wildest dreams.

We arrived at the farm and I pulled the car around to the front of the house. Skip was sitting on the porch sipping on a tall glass of ice water. Even though it was early, it looked like he had just finished putting in a full day's work. Skip stood up from his rocking chair and put on his broken pair of glasses as my car pulled up to his porch. Skip walked down the front steps and over to my car. I watched his facial expression transform from confusion to joy, as he caught a glimpse of his son sitting on the passenger side of my car.

"My bouy! Marco is that you? " Skip yelled as he opened the passenger side door. I would assume Skip probably doesn't watch much television or visit websites like TMZ or Huffington post. Hell, he probably doesn't even know the internet exists. In any event, Skip had no clue his son was alive.

Skip grabbed Marco's arm and pulled him out of the car.

"It's a miracle o' lawd' my bouy's alive!"

Marco stood there, slouched over in front of his dad, like one of those zombies from the Walking Dead.

"What's the matta' with ma' boy?" Skip said as he looked into Marco's lifeless eyes.

"I…. killed…. her. I…. killed…. her. I…. killed…. her."

"Killed who son? You done gone mad. Like Rusty when he done caught rabies from dat' fox, back when you was a youngin'."

Skip grabbed Marco and began shaking him. I had to jump in, because the old man looked like he was trying to shake the crazy out of Marco.

"Mr. Skip, Marco's not doing too good. We have to get him to the sunflower meadow."

"Why's that? First I thought my bouy' was dead? Now he done come back crazay?"

I explained the entire situation to Skip about how Marco was held hostage all this time and was not killed in a car accident. I also explained how the meadow could be the trigger to getting Marco's mind back. I could see the wheels turning in Skips head as he began to understand the importance of getting Marco to the sunflower meadow.

"let's get my bouy' to the meadow!" Skip said with a hint of a smile. Skip and I walked a zombiefied Marco past the field of blueberries and up the small mountain behind the barn. We all stood at the edge of the mountain above the meadow of sunflowers. The last time I was here I dreamed of one day sharing this with Marco. Today my dream came true, well kinda'.

"Marco we're here."

I held Marco's hand as his head slowly raised. The sun illuminated the entire meadow as a flock of cardinals danced from flower to flower. The meadow was so beautiful. It was as picturesque as I remembered it. I could see a hint of recognition come over Marco's face as he walked to the edge of the small mountain. Before I could utter another word, he ran down the side of the mountain and down into the meadow. He looked like a little boy returning home after being away on a long trip. I followed behind Marco as he jumped for joy.

Halfway through his run, Marco stopped in the middle of the meadow. Thank God he did because I was out of breath trying to catch up with him. I could see a look of recognition come over Marco's face as he approached the awkward looking table set in the middle of the meadow. I recognized the table too. It was the table Skip set for my imaginary date with Marco. Marco walked up to the table and sat down on one of the chairs.

"I killed her…. I killed her…. I killed her" Marco repeated as he rocked back and forth in his chair. I sat down at the table next to him and tried to think of what to do next. The meadow wasn't working. If anything it was making Marco worse. Oh goodness, I didn't know what to do next. I had to find a way to break Marco's trance.

Before I could get the thought through my mind. I saw Marco's letter sitting on the ground near the table. I had to do a double take. *How in the world did this get here?* I thought to myself. I don't know if it was divine intervention or dumb luck, but I reached down and picked up the letter. I sat as close as I could to Marco and I began to read it to him.

My dear Sarah

I hope you're enjoying my meadow of sunflowers. I built this in memory of my real mother. There were some mornings I would leave home before dawn. I was coming here to cultivate this meadow. I know you were worried and Lord knows I hope you didn't think I was seeing another woman. I was coming here. I have a tough time talking about this, plus what tough macho military guy wants to tell anyone he's working on a meadow of sunflowers?

I watched as Marco's body stopped rocking. He turned around in his seat and stared at me. It looked like it was working, so I kept reading.

I was raised on this farm with my mother and father until I was twelve years old. I hated this farm for years and I prayed one day we would move to the city. My mother used to beg me all the time to stop dreaming of the city and help her build a meadow of flowers. She wanted a place of her own. A place away from the cows and the chickens. A place where she could sit and just enjoy being alive. My mom had really bad arthritis and towards the end she could barely walk, so she needed my help to build the meadow. I was a stupid kid back then and didn't want any part in building a meadow. Every free chance I got I would ride my bike into town to play basketball. I had no time for flower picking. One day my mom decided she had enough of begging me to help, so she decided to cultivate the meadow of flowers herself.

"Mom wanted a meadow…. Mom wanted a meadow…. Mom wanted a meadow." Marco repeated while tears poured down his cheeks.

On her way up the mountain to the meadow, she slipped and fell on a large bolder. My mom landed pretty hard. It breaks my heart because my mom was out there unconscious in this meadow all by herself. It would be several hours before we found her. By the time we did find her it was too late. My mother was gone.

"We buried my mother…. right… right.. here in the meadow. I built this in her memory." Marco said calmly. For the first time since I met him, Marco was making sense.

There hasn't been a day in my life where I don't feel guilty for her death. If I just helped her instead of being a knuckle head, she would be alive today. We buried my mom in this meadow. After her death times got dark and hard for me. I couldn't take the guilt anymore so my dad let me leave the farm. He sent me to live with my aunt and uncle in the city. I love my auntie and uncle because they raised me as their own but they will never fill the void that was left when my mom died. My mother's favorite flower is the sunflower and that's what I chose for this meadow. You are now the only person outside of my family that knows this story. For years I felt I had to deal with this alone. I punished myself because of it and I didn't want to put that burden on you.

This picnic basket is filled with peanut butter and jelly sandwiches. I know it not a big and fancy dinner but this was my favorite meal as a kid. My mom would make them for me all the time. So please sit back and enjoy. And know that I love you and I am happy I can finally share this with you. I'm sorry I hid this from you and please forgive me and understand......

I looked up from the letter, Marco was staring at me intently. I looked him in the eyes as I read the last sentence of his letter.

I love you!

Marco

Marco smiled. It felt good to see him happy. After all that he's been through, a smile was a major breakthrough.

I was about to get up from my chair and give Marco a hug when his body began shaking uncontrollably.

"MARCO!" I screamed loudly.

Marco began gasping for air as his eyes rolled to the back of his head. It looked like he was about to fall to the ground as he wobbled back and forth in his chair. I jumped up from my seat and ran over to him as fast as I could.

"MARCO, NO!" I didn't get there in enough time. Marco fell out of his chair and onto the ground, his body twitching and his mouth foaming.

"MARCO! MARCO! MARCO!" I screamed, as I tried to wake him. Marco was unresponsive, his eyes moving back and forth behind his closed eye lids as he lay on the ground amongst the sunflowers.

"HE'S HAVING SOME SORT OF SEIZURE OR SOMETHING!" I yelled out in the empty meadow. I was frantic and had no idea what to do, so I held Marco. I held him tight in my arms and rocked him back and forth.

Skip must have heard my screams because I could see the old man running towards us with a pitcher of ice water in his hands. It looked sort of strange but I had no time to question it. As he approached, Skip poured the entire pitcher of ice water over Marco's head.

"SON, WAKE UP!" Skip yelled as he stood up over Marco and I. As if jolted by lightning, Marco jumped up from my lap and rolled over on his back. I looked on in awe as he slowly opened his eyes. He sat up and looked around, confused.

"Where.. am I?" Marco asked as he shook the cold water from his face and hair.

"You're home, bouy'" Skip answered.

"Home, how did I get here?" Marco looked confused as he looked back and forth between me and his father.

"The last thing…. I remember was being…. in a cave!"

"Marco you're free. You're home in your mother's meadow."

Marco looked at me confused. Like he was seeing me for the first time.

"And… who are you?"

"She's yo' wife, son." Skip replied.

Marco looked even more confused. I had to come clean with the truth.

"Well, I'm not really your wife. My name is Nia." I said as I extended my hand to Marco. Marco shook my hand as Skip looked down at me with a confused / angry glare. I felt bad for lying to Skip, but I was caught up in the moment. I was a woman looking for love and Marco's letters were the remedy.

"So…who are you Nia… and did you bring me here?" Marco struggle to say.

I looked deep into Marco's eyes. He was back. The trance was broken. I took a deep breath before answering. How in the world was I was going to explain all of this to him? So much had happened. Lord only knows what I've been through.

"To make a long story short. You and I were in a tragic car accident that supposedly killed you. My lungs ruptured in the accident and I was given your lungs. Obviously, you weren't really killed because you're standing right here in front of us. Come to find out you were actually being held hostage by a terrorist group." I blurted out.

I hated to be blunt, but I had to let Marco and Skip know the truth.

"Did you just say you were given my lungs?"

"Well, I guess they weren't your lungs because you're kind of using YOUR lungs right now." I said sarcastically.

Marco walked over to me and placed his hands on my shoulders. I could see a look of concern with a hint of fear in his eyes. I felt like he was about to tell me I had a week to live or something horrible like that.

"Nia, did they tell you the lungs you received were mine?" Marco repeated slowly.

"Yes, they did." I said nervously.

Marco closed his eyes and rubbed his forehead.

"Fuck! They must've found out!" Marco uttered.

"Found out what?" Marco was starting to scare me.

"Who are "THEY" and what did they find out?"

Marco took a deep breath before he answered.

"If they thought it was me that died in that crash and they think they gave you my lungs… Oh God, Nia you're in danger."

"In what? What do you mean?"

I watched Marco's eyes squint and his brow curl as he gripped my arm tightly.

"They don't care about you, Nia. They want the microchip on your lungs. "What do you mean?" I responded as my body shook uncontrollably. Marco paused and looked me deep in my eyes.

"They want that microchip on your lungs and they are going to kill you to get it."

CHAPTER 7: THE MOST POWERFUL MAN IN THE WORLD

None of this made any sense. Why would someone want to kill me? I could feel an uneasiness come over my body. What in the world did I get myself into?

I looked at Marco, hoping his eyes would reveal this was all some sort of cruel joke. I prayed his smile would provide some comfort. There would be no smile, just a look of seriousness in Marco's eyes. If I could rewind my life a year, I would. The stress of being an Executive and planning a wedding was nothing compared to being told you have a microchip in your body and someone wants to kill you to get it.

"What's on my lungs Marco? Who are THEY and why are THEY trying to kill me?" I demanded. The questions were pouring out of me like a faucet. Marco grabbed my hand and took a deep breath. By the look in his eyes, I could tell the news wasn't going to be good.

"You have a microchip on your lungs that is barely visible to the naked eye. There is a video on this chip that some very important people desperately want to get their hands on."

"They want to kill me over a stupid video?"

"Nia, It's not just any ordinary video. It's a video of the most powerful man in the world doing things he is not supposed to be doing."

"The most powerful man in the world? I have a video of the President on my lungs?"

Marco frowned as if annoyed by the suggestion.

"Bigger than the president. Nia, this is some serious stuff. This man controls the entire world. The President answers to him, even though the

President doesn't know it. The decisions this man makes affects entire nations, Europe, Asia, Africa, the Americas, Australia… you name it he controls it."

"Does this microchip have spy video on it or something?"
It was the only thing I could think of that would make the most powerful man in the world want to kill a harmless woman. Marco paused for a moment before answering. I could tell he didn't want to reveal top secret information to a woman he just met five minutes ago, but the microchip was in my body and I had every right to know.

"Have you ever heard of a company called Vista Visions?"
My heart dropped. *Vista Visions?* That was the last thing I expected to come out of Marco's mouth.

"Yes, I heard of them. I work for them… well I mean I used to work for them."

Marco looked confused. He looked me up and down as if he was trying to decide if he should trust me or not.

"You used to work for Vista Visions?"
"Yes, I was their VP of Marketing."

"Then you know a lot about the company?"
"I hope so, I ran their entire marketing division. Their security software is on 50% of the computers in the United States." I responded.

With my time at Vista Visions, the company grew into one of the largest companies in the world, and turned Bo Vista and his evil wife, Katy into Trillionairs. You can't watch TV or surf the internet without seeing one of my commercials, boasting how Vista Visions has the safest most un-hackable security software in the world.

"50% of the computers? Yeah right. Their software is on more like 95% of the computers across the globe and most people don't even realize they are using it." Marco replied.

"This didn't make any sense. I've seen the numbers, I've done the market analysis myself. Our software is not on that many computers." Marco looked a bit relieved. Apparently, I was clueless of Vista Visions illegal activity.

"Even with your high position in the company, I can tell you have no idea what Bo Vista has going on behind closed doors. We are talking about bribes, blackmail, controlling governments and using their software to spy on every person on this planet. They have dirt on everybody."

The news was shocking. I really respect Bo. In all my years of working for him, he was a hardworking man who turned nothing into something. Our software system is his baby and he is very passionate about protecting the security of the world. It didn't make any sense. Why would he use his baby to spy on people?

"So what does all of this have to do with the chip on my lungs?" Marco took a deep breath. He had a paranoid look on his face as he scanned the meadow for anyone else besides us who could be listening.

"There is a video on that microchip of Bo and his wife, Katy, doing things that should never leave the privacy of a husband and his wife's bedroom. If you know what I mean."

"You mean to tell me I have video of Bo and Katy Vista getting "freaky" on my lungs?" Marco looked annoyed by my joke. He got a little closer and began to whisper.

"If this video ever got out. It would ruin them! Nia, I will explain more later. Right now I have to get you out of here. It's not safe."

Marco gave his father a look and asked him if the barn was still there. Skip gave Marco a wink as he reached in his pants pocket and pulled out a set of keys and handed them to Marco.

"You take care of this gurl', son!" Skip commanded.

"I will dad."

Marco grabbed my hand and guided me across the sunflower field. We were headed to this mysterious barn.

CHAPTER 8: SAFE HOUSE

My heart was beating fast as the adrenaline pumped through my veins. Marco's revelation and his sense of urgency was scaring the living shit out of me! I had a microchip on my lungs and somebody was trying to kill me to get it! *Marco baby, I needed more answers!* But I had no time to focus on any of this, because Marco had my hand and was guiding me to the rundown red barn behind the sunflower meadow.

The barn was old and raggedy. It looked like a strong gust of wind could easily blow it over. A rusty but strong chain with a giant pad lock secured the front doors. I struggled to catch my breath as Marco removed Skip's key ring from his back pocket. He placed a gold key with the initials "ARS" engraved on it, into the padlock. *What in the world could Marco and his father have in this old barn that would require it to be padlocked? Maybe it held a motorcycle or some old muscle car Marco could use to whisk me off to safety. Whatever was in this barn they wanted to keep it top secret.*

Once the chain was off, I nervously followed Marco into the old barn. It smelled old and musty inside, like no one had been inside it in years. Beyond that, it looked like a typical barn (At least to the eyes of a city girl like me). There were dried up bales of hay, garden tools, a horse stable and two broken down tractor trailers. Damn, no signs of a motorcycle or a fantasy muscle car.

Marco grabbed my hand and guided me over to one of the vacant horse stables. This may be my chance to ride off into my dreams on a black stallion with Marco, my black stallion.

Once inside the stable, Marco let go of my hand and then dropped down to his knees and began frantically brushing aside the hay that lay on the stable floor. *Marco, what are you doing?* He looked like a mad man searching for a needle in a hay stack.

With the hay brushed aside, Marco looked up into my eyes and smiled. He found what he was looking for. I stood frozen. The sunlight oozing through a hole in the roof of the barn, glistened over his muscular shoulders. Damn, he was so fucking sexy! *Nia, get it together, girl!*

Marco grabbed on to a metal door handle attached to the floor. He tugged hard on the handle several times, revealing a hidden door on the floor of the stable.

"What in the world?" I said aloud.

Marco looked back at me and smiled again, right before he pried the door open and motioned me to follow him through. *Oh no, I hope he doesn't expect me to follow him in there!* There were nasty cobwebs hanging all over the door. I guarantee you there was a nasty black spider just waiting to pounce on me, once I walked through it. *Oh, hell no!*

Marco extended his hand, so I guess I had no choice but to follow. He led me down an old staircase that opened up to a dark room. I had one hand on the wall and the other in the comfort of Marco's hand as we both searched the wall for a light switch. "CLICK" the light switch sounded as the lights flickered all around us.

I don't know what I expected to find down there, but I can tell you what I wasn't expecting…..a hi-tech bomb shelter!

There was a bunk bed and a computer desk and chair in the corner of the large room. On the back wall there were large shelves filled with canned goods and bottles of water. This hi-tech underground bunker had a small kitchen and bathroom along with several walls filled with televisions and computer monitors displaying exterior views of the farm, all of the necessities of a high tech command center.

Marco opened a large cabinet in the corner of the room. I walked over to get a closer look. The cabinet had an entire arsenal of hand guns, machine guns, knives, swords, and grenades. You name the weapon, it was in this cabinet. Marco grabbed a small black hand gun and placed it in his waist band.

"Who in the world are you and what is this place?"

"It's a safe house for emergencies." Marco replied.

I have to admit, there was something creepy and sexy about all of this.

"Nia, you will be safe here until I get back."

"Get back? Where are you going? You can't leave me here."

"Nia, I need to get you to a safer place. Once they find out where you are, they are going to try to kill you. I need to get to Sarge and his helicopter. We will fly you to another safe house until we can figure things out."

Safe houses, guns, microchips all of this sounded so crazy. WTF is going on? I reached in my back pocket and removed my cellphone.

"Here, why don't you call Sarge from my phone?"

It only made sense. Why go through all of this top secret stuff? When a simple phone call and Sarge is a helicopter ride away. Plus, there is no way I was going to stay in this creepy bunker all by myself. Marco looked down at my cellphone and then back up to me.

"Cell phones aren't safe, Nia. They can track them. I need to talk to Sarge face to face. That's the safest way."

Marco must have seen the horror in my eyes, because his face quickly transformed from "soldier save the world" mode to "everything's going to be o.k." mode.

"Nia, I promise I won't be gone long. You didn't ask to be in this. They want to kill you because of me. It's my fault and I vow to take care of you, even if it kills me!" *Ugh, Marco has a way of giving me the chills.* This is the Marco I knew from his love letters. This is the Marco I had fallen in love with. The Marco that would do anything for the woman he loved. He makes me feel safe and I trust him. I didn't want to stay in this bunker, but I knew I had to, at least until Marco came back with Sarge.

Marco walked over to the gun cabinet. I guess one gun wasn't enough. Marco began rifling through the cabinet until he came upon a shiny silver handgun. Marco took the gun off of the rack and handed it over to me. *What, huh? Did I miss something?* I swallowed hard, clearing my dry throat as I took the gun from Marco's hand.

"What do you want me to do with this?"
The gun felt ice cold and heavy in my hands. This is the first time I've ever held a gun. It was heavier than it looked. I looked down at the piece of steel. I had the power in my hands to take someone's life. I don't know if I necessarily wanted that kind of power.

"Nia, if anyone comes through that door that is not me or my father, I want you to use this. Have you ever used one of these before?"
I looked at Marco like he was crazy. "I am a business executive not a killer!"

"Well, you just hold it at your target and squeeze. It's just that simple." Marco said as he demonstrated with his hands.

Goodness, if someone really did come through that door, I planned to hide. Using this gun would be my last option.

"So, whose lungs are in my body? If they're not yours, then whose are they?" It was an awkward question and probably the wrong time, but I needed more answers.

Marco paused and put down his hands before answering. He made a promise to give me more answers and I was not going to let him leave me here without knowing more. Marco closed his eyes and took a deep breath.

"Nia, the lungs aren't mine." Marco professed.

"Well, I kind of assumed that." I responded. Marco smiled and of course my heart melted a little bit.

"Nia, the lungs in your body belong to a soldier named Jessie Acuna. He's was a fellow Marine and a great friend. Jess and I go way back, back to the days of boot camp, about twenty years ago." *Jessie Acuna? Who the hell is that?* I thought to myself.

"You see, a few months ago, I was on my last tour of duty and I was put in charge of a private security detail to guard two news reporters who were in Khaberistan to interview Bo and Katy Vista."

"Bo and Katy Vista!? I just can't keep them out of my life!"

Marco continued…."Bo and Katy were in the Europe selling their new software to the Khaberistanian government. I'm not sure if you know, Khaberistan is a hotbed of terrorist activity. The M.A.I.O are rumored to be headquartered in this region. I was only a few days away from heading back to the States for good. I had just gotten married and I was looking forward to coming home to be with my new wife. I didn't want any part of this detail."

I know you were coming home. I read the love letters you wrote to that crazy bitch! I said to myself behind a fake smile. If Marco only knew what that muscle bound crazy ass wife of his was doing with their neighbor Todd, while he was gone protecting our country, he would flip.

Marco continued…. "It was a simple assignment for easy money. All I had to do was escort two news reporters to the house Bo and Katy Vista were renting in Khaberistan. The news reporters would interview Bo about his software and how it will help modernize the Khaberistan government and help fight terrorism. Something didn't feel right about this detail, so I went with my gut and backed out of it. All I wanted to do was get home to my Sarah." *She's not your Sarah, she's Todd's!* I could feel my jaw tightening as Marco continued his story.

"That's when my buddy Jess jumped in and begged me to give him the assignment. His wife at home was pregnant with twins and he needed the extra money. I let Jess know he couldn't take the assignment because it required top level security clearance and I was the only one authorized to work the detail. That's when Jess came up with the crazy idea of using my identity for the detail. Fuck! That should have been Jess in the cave and me in the car accident!"

I watched Marco's eyes turn red. He was riled with guilt for switching identities with Jess.

"I should have told Jess no when he asked to switch fucking dog tags! I'm so fucking stupid! He's got twins at home who are never going to meet their father!"

I leaned in and gave Marco a hug. It was the only way I knew to comfort him. I felt so guilty for making him dig up his past. Marco held me tight. Then he took a deep breath and continued his story.

"When Jess got back the next morning he looked scared as hell. He told me he was afraid for his life and that he found a way to make millions and retire from the service for good. Jess was always trying to find ways to get rich quick and I think he thought he found his golden ticket."

"Oh no, what did Jess find?" I replied.

"Jess said the interview ran late so Katy Vista invited Jess and the news reporters to stay the night in the home they were renting. It was late and too dangerous to drive in Khaberistan at night, so Jess and the reporters agreed to stay and drive back to the base the next morning. This was when things got ugly. After a late night of heavy drinking, Jess "happened" to stumble upon the Vista's private bedroom. Jess told me he could hear all kinds of moaning and groaning going on inside.

Oh boy, this is getting juicy!

"Their bedroom door was partially open so Jess decided to take a peek inside. By the sounds of the moans, Jess was expecting to find Bo and Katy getting it on." Marco explained.

"Is that what was happening? Is that what he found?" I asked. Marco grinned slightly as he continued to explain.

"Not quite, however his guess was pretty close. There was someone else in the room with the Vista's."

"What? What? What? There was someone else in the room with them!?" Marco chuckled at my response.

"Oh yeah, The Vista's were fully engaged in a threesome with another man." Marco responded.

"Oh my God, this is crazy! Wait until Harley hears this!"

This news was scandalous! Like something right out of the show Love and Hip hop or Real Housewives of Atlanta. I knew there was something off with Katy! Not only did I want this chip off of my lungs. I also wanted to see who was in this video with the Vista's.

"So who's having a ménage a trios' with the Vista's?

Marco grabbed a hold of my shoulder to break me from my "scandalous, I got gossip to tell, trance" so he could inform me of the seriousness of the issue at hand.

"Nia, you can't mention this to anyone! Having a threesome is one thing, but this ménage a trios would destroy their business and get them sent to prison for treason, if the public found out who they were in bed with! Jess being Jess, he immediately saw dollars signs. So what did Jess do?"

"Oh no, he videotaped it, didn't he?" I responded.

"That's right. Jess recorded it with his mobile phone."

"So how in the world did this video get on a microchip?"

"Nia, this is classified info so this conversation I am having with you never happened." Marco cautioned before he continued.

"The U.S government smuggles all types of top secret information in and out of different foreign countries. In order for it to go undetected, often times they will implant the information on a microchip inside the bodies of one of their covert op soldiers. If the soldier ever gets caught or killed by the enemy, the information goes undetected." *Ok, this story is getting crazier!*

Marco continued… "When Jess returned to our base the next

morning he had one of our Medics implant the video on a microchip and then implant it on his lungs. It's a quick minor surgery. Jess has had it done numerous times. His dumb plan was to bring the video home and sell it to TMZ or one of the other tabloids. The video would ruin Bo Vista and make Jess a millionaire."

Curiosity was getting the best of me. I could only imagine who in the world would be in bed with Bo and Katy. Bo didn't seem like the type to share his wife with another man, but Katy on the other hand, I wouldn't put anything past her. I imagined it to be some celebrity or some big politician in bed with the Vista's. It had to be someone who was big enough and important enough to make them want to kill.

"So who were they sleeping with?" I asked. I knew Marco and his "top secret" covert ops mind would never tell me, but hell, the video is in my body and I have a right to know!

"Nia, you know I can't tell you. It's confidential information. I have already told you more than I should. It could get me court marshalled."

Once again, this was all so surreal. I was waiting for Marco to laugh and say this was some sort of cruel April fool's joke. Stuff like this never happens in my boring ass life.

"I'm still confused. You were the one identified in the traffic accident not Jess." I asked.

"Well, things happened so fast that morning. Jess got the implant as soon as he got back to base. Two days later the same news reporters needed an escort to another military base several hundred miles away so they could fly back to the U.S.

After some serious begging from Jess, I agreed to ride with him to escort the reporters to the other base. He feared for his life and wanted me to watch his back. Plus, he wasn't exactly one hundred percent after his surgery implant." *Marco, is a great man. He supported his friend regardless of the situation.* I smiled at my man as he continued his story.

"There must have been a leak or Jess must have bragged about what he saw that night, because Kathy and Bo Vista found out that the soldier (Marco Silver), who spent the evening at their rented home in Khaberistan had video of the Vista's little tryst. I know Bo was pissed. This video would destroy him. I also know Bo would be willing to do any and everything in his power to destroy the video before it leaked out to the public."

This was shocking news. *I couldn't imagine Bo Vista behind any of this. He wouldn't harm a fly.*

Marco continued…"I had an eerie feeling the entire ride up to the other base. My feelings were confirmed when our military jeep was ambushed by insurgents. They came out of nowhere. The guys were dressed in all black and carried heavy machine guns. They covered their faces to conceal their identities, however, I could tell they were part of the M.A.I.O. These weren't some hired Guerillas, these men were trained killers.

"Oh my God Marco, what did you do?"
"Jess and I were not going to get captured and become part of some terrorist assassination or hostage situation, so we did what we were trained to do. We fired on the insurgents!

Unfortunately, they fired back and eventually destroyed our jeep and wounded one of the reporters. Nia, there were just too many of them! We were dead to rights. If it weren't for the civilian reporters we were protecting, I would have kept fighting until my last breath!" *Oh Marco!*

"We all hid behind our burning jeep as the bullets from the insurgents guns whizzed by our heads. Of course, Jess being Jess, he got scared and ran off into the desert. I did what any good soldier would do for his brother. I sent cover fire, so Jess could escape. He needed to get back home to his wife and his twins. I understood.

The news reporters and I weren't so lucky. I had a duty to protect them and that's exactly what I did....I protected them by surrendering.

We were captured, tortured and held hostage in a cave by the M.A.I.O for what felt like years. I didn't fully understand why they didn't just kill us during the ambush. It was when the M.A.I.O started torturing me and trying to find information on Marco Silver, I realized I was still wearing Jess's dog tags. They thought I was Jesse. The insurgents knew "Marco Silver" was supposed to be in the jeep and they assumed the soldier who escaped was him. It is my duty to give them no information and that was what I did, despite being tortured."

Marco paused and looked down at his boots. I could tell the memories and wounds from his torture were still very fresh. Marco lifted his head and put on a forced smile as he continued to explain.

"Jess did make it home with the microchip, but he didn't get too far. He was killed in a car accident as soon as he got back to the States. Coincidence, I don't think so."

"After the car accident, shouldn't Jess's dental and medical records prove he wasn't you? The records wouldn't match." I asked.

"It should have, I bet Sarge pulled some strings and had our medical records switched. Sarge is a specialist. This is the type of stuff he does. He was trying to protect me. I was considered safe, if I was dead."

It all kind of making sense, in a weird sort of way. Although I still needed more answers. Did Marco know about the weird freckled killer and most importantly how do I get this chip off of my lungs?

"Nia, I promise I will explain more, but right now time is not on our side. I have to get to Sarge so we can get you to a safer place."

I wasn't fully satisfied, but I had enough information to hold me off until Marco returned and could explain more. I took a deep breath and held the gun tightly in my hand as Marco walked out of the bunker and closed the door behind him. Crazy thoughts ran through my mind as I sat in the bunker, alone and afraid.

How in the world am I going to explain this to Terence? What about my family?" I can't just disappear and go into hiding without letting anyone know.

I sat down in the leather office chair in front of all of the video monitors. I could see the entire farm from several different angles. I watched Marco get into an old beat up faded red pickup truck and speed off of the farm. I felt myself sigh as I tried to absorb it all in.

Marco, my dreams about you were never like this!

In my mind, I tried to put the pieces of this weird puzzle together. The microchip and the video would explained the freckled killer that was following me around. He must have been hired to…. kill me. Never in my wildest dreams would I have thought I would be the target of a crazed killer. It all seemed unreal. I can't believe Bo hired someone to kill Jess.

My thoughts were interrupted by a slight buzzing sound.

"WHAT IN THE WORLD IS THAT!" I screamed as I raised my

gun towards the bunker door. "BUZZZZZZZ" *There it goes again!*

I was about to go full Rambo when I realized it was my cellphone vibrating in my back pocket. "Oh God!" I said aloud as I pulled my phone from my pocket. I looked down at the phone. It was a call from Terence. I had quite a few missed calls as well, several from my mother and two from Terence. The underground bunker must have killed my phone signal.

I was tempted to answer the phone and tell Terence exactly what was going on, but I knew it wouldn't be safe if I answered. I watched nervously with each ring and breathed a sigh of relief when my phone went to voice mail. *Ok good, let me check the message.*

As soon as I lifted a finger to check, the phone began buzzing again. It was Terence again. *Goodness I need to answer! I need to talk to Terence. I could use him right now!* I fought the temptation and put the phone back down on the desk. *Focus Nia, Focus.*

The phone wasn't out of my hands for more than two seconds when I received a text message from Terence. I picked up the phone and clicked on the text message.

FROM TERENCE: Nia where are you? Pick up the phone! It's an emergency!!

I gazed down at the words on my phone, nervously. *"Emergency"* Oh *goodness! I have to text him back. I wonder if a text can be tracked?*
I put the phone back down on the desk. *Ignore it Nia. Ignore it!*

I knew if I answered it, I could put all of the lives of the people I love in jeopardy. Terence's can be dramatic sometimes, maybe this was just a ploy to get me to answer. The phone's buzz echoed again on the desk. It was another text from Terence.

FROM TERENCE: It's Abony. Please call me when you get this!!!

Abony? What's wrong with Abony? I took a deep breath and picked up my phone. I planned to keep the call brief. *If I'm not on the phone for a long time, maybe I can't be traced. Well, that's at least how it works in the movies.*

My hand was shaking as I dialed. I kept hitting the wrong numbers. *Get it together Nia, get it together!* I had no idea what Terence was going to tell me about Abony. I put the phone on speaker and listened to it ring on the other end.

"Nia, is that you?" Terence voice echoed over the phones speakers.

"Yes."

"Where are you?"

"Terence, I can't talk right now. What's up with Abony?"

I could hear Terence take a deep breath. He was starting to scare me.

"Nia, I'm in Abony's apartment." Terence voiced cracked as he spoke. He sounded frantic.

"What are you doing there?"

"Your mother called me and asked me to check on Abony."

Check on Abony? None of this made any kind of sense.

"Why would my mother want you to check on Abony?"

"Nia, I don't know what to do." Terence responded nervously.

"Terence, what do you mean? Where is Abony and why did my mother call you?"

There was dead silence on the other end of the phone.

"TERENCE! What's going on?"

65

"Oh my God Nia, there's blood everywhere!"

"Blood? Terence what's going on?"

Terence sounded like he was in shock. He wasn't making any sense.

"Terence... where... is... Abony?" I said slowly, praying I could get through to him.

"Nia, Abony is missing."

"What do you mean missing?" I answered.

"Andy's foster mother called your mother looking for Andy. She said Abony was late and she threatened to call Abony's Case Worker if Andy was not returned in an hour. Your mother called me because she couldn't find you. So I told her I would go by Abony's apartment and see if everything was o.k."

"Was she there?" I asked... not really wanting to hear the answer. Terence took another deep breath.

"Nia, Abony's not here."

"Did you try calling her phone? Maybe she took Andy out for lunch. She can't be missing, it's not like her." I prayed Abony wasn't stupid enough to try to skip town with Andy. If she did and got caught she would lose him forever.

"Nia, I pray Abony is JUST missing." Terence responded.

"What?" Why would Terence pray Abony was "just missing." He wasn't making any sense.

"Nia, when I got to Abony's apartment her front door was kicked open. I got scared so I called the police."

"Oh God!" I clutched my phone tightly.

"Nia, I walked inside to see what was going on. There is blood

66

everywhere! Oh God Nia, it's all over her walls, floors and kitchen counters!

Oh goodness! What in the world is going on? Blood? I pray nothing happened to Abony or Andy.

"What about Andy? Oh God is Andy there?"

"I didn't find Abony or Andy, just blood, Nia. There was some sort of a struggle." The phone went dead silent.

"Terence are you still there?"

"Nia, I think this is Abony and Andy's blood."

I kept hearing Terence's words over and over in my head.

"I think this is Abony and Andy's blood."

"I think this is Abony and Andy's blood."

"I think this is Abony and Andy's blood."

"I think this is Abony and Andy's blood."

"NIA, are you there?" Terence's voice broke my trance as I began to wipe the tears from my face. *I have to get myself together. I have to get to Abony's apartment and I had to get there now!* I kept shifting my focus to the positive. *They were still alive if their bodies weren't found. Oh God! I can't believe I'm thinking about Abony an Andy like this!* I could feel myself beginning to cry again.

"Focus Nia, focus!" I said to myself.

I put myself at risk for making the phone call and I know Marco told me not to leave the farm, but I have to leave. Abony and Andy's lives depend on it. I pray I'm not too late! I tucked the gun in my waistband and rushed out of the bunker door.

CHAPTER 9: POOL OF BLOOD

I got in my car and drove as fast as I could. I had no time to worry about my phone call being traced. If someone was coming to kill me, then they will have to get in line. Right now, finding Abony and Andy is my only priority. I have no time to be dead. I left Marco a note on the table in the bunker, telling him where I was going and why I left. I know, it's not what he wanted but I know he will understand. I left him Abony's address and my telephone number just in case. I know he won't call, but I didn't want to leave him high and dry. When this is all said and done, I know I will need his protection.

I arrived on Abony's street. The entire ride was one fast blur. I don't think I took my foot off the gas pedal the entire ride. Terence's car was parked in front of Abony's apartment. I breathed a sigh of relief, the police had not arrived yet. That's not a big surprise in this neighborhood. Police are never in a rush to come to the rescue of a coke addicted ex stripper living in subsidized housing. Then again, Abony could have been a nurse with a husband and child and there still wouldn't have been a big rush to come to her rescue. This was a neighborhood the world had forgotten, written off, hopeless.

I parked my car behind Terence's. I was out of the car and up the flight of stairs to Abony's apartment before my car actually stopped rolling. I honestly don't remember if I put the car in park. Everything was a big blur.

I stopped in my tracks when I arrived at Abony's front door. The sight of large black boot prints smeared across Abony's front door sent chills up my spine. This was for real. This wasn't happening to some unknown face on a news report. This was Abony's front door. I grabbed the door handle and the door almost fell off the hinges. Someone definitely forced their way into my sister's apartment. I took a deep breath and contemplated turning around and getting back in my car. I was so afraid of what I was going to find in Abony's apartment. I gathered my courage and pushed the front door open. I knew my fear was only going to delay the inevitable. I walked into the living room.

Terence was standing in the middle of the chaos with both of his hands on his head. He looked like a lost child wandering the mall in search of his missing parents. I know Terence had warned me about the blood, but it didn't prepare me for what I saw in Abony's apartment. You could never be prepared for something like this. Abony's apartment looked like a crime scene. Her living room sofa was turned upside down and stained with bright red blood. There were bloody hand prints all over the kitchen cabinets and walls. The glass coffee table that was once the resting place of Abony's favorite magazines, was thrown on the opposite side of the room and shattered into a million pieces and the flat screen TV my mother bought Abony for Christmas was torn from the wall and lying on the living room floor.

Despite all of the mess, my attention was drawn to the giant pool of blood resting in the center of the living room. I walked up behind Terence and tapped him on the shoulder. Terence jumped, he didn't even realize I walked into the room.

"Oh God, Nia. You scared me."
Terence rubbed his hand through his scruffy beard and looked at me with

puffy swollen eyes. He must've been crying.

"I've never seen this much blood in my life and I'm a surgeon."

"Oh God Terence, do you think they're ok?"

Terence took a deep breath, avoiding eye contact. He didn't have to say it because I already knew his answer. It was written all over his face.

"Did you look all over the apartment?"

I was grabbing at straws, hoping Terence didn't search the entire apartment, maybe Abony and Andy were hiding under a bed or in a closet. Terence looked me in the eyes. I've never seen him this scared in my life.

"Nia, I looked everywhere. They're not here."

"Do you think their ......?"

I couldn't even say the word. My sister is a knucklehead, but I love her. I would die if something ever happened to her and my nephew. Terence gave me a hug. His embrace was a temporary relief as I rested the side of my face on his chest. I wish I could just stay in his arms forever, and make all of this go away. If I could, I would never ever leave his arms. As Terence held me, I prayed Abony was ok. I couldn't imagine having to tell my mother something happened to Abony and Andy. It would absolutely kill her. My mind started searching for answers. Who would do something like this? My sister wouldn't harm a fly and my poor nephew Andy, it seems he can never catch a break in life.

I forced myself to shake it all off as I tried to regain my focus. I couldn't help Abony if I'm sitting here sulking. I walked over to the pool of blood and looked around for any evidence that could help me figure out what had gone on here. As I examined the pool of blood, I noticed a small blood trail trickling from the corner of the blood pool. I got down on my knees to get a closer look. The blood trail looked like a pair of child size footprints. They had to be Andy's shoe prints. They were too small to be Abony's or any other adult's. I followed the trail to the back bedroom. The prints faded a bit, however they led me right to Abony's bed. I got down on my knees, took a deep breath and prayed for the best.

I hoped I would find Andy hiding underneath the bed, safe and sound. I poked my head under the bed and was disappointed. Andy wasn't there. All I found was a pair of child size bloody hand prints, staining the carpet underneath the bed. The prints were bright red in one spot, then they slowly faded as they smeared to the other side of the bed. Oh God! It looked like Andy was hiding under the bed and someone reached underneath and grabbed his ankles and pulled him out from underneath the bed. I put my hands over my mouth and tried to hold my composure. Whatever went on in the living room, Andy must have witnessed it.

I ran back to the pool of blood in the center of the living room. There had to be some other type of evidence or clue in the living room that could help me find out who took my sister and nephew. The police would be here any minute now and I needed some answers.

Terence had opened the window blinds in the living room to add some sunlight to the dark and dreary room. With the sun peering through the window, something in the pool of blood caught my attention. It was small, shiny and sitting in the middle of the pool. It was hard to see in the dark, however the reflecting sun made it obvious. I bent over to get a better look. It looked like some sort of gold chain. I didn't want to tamper with the scene or have my fingerprints inside the blood pool, so with the tips of my fingers, I reached over and pulled the chain out from the pool of blood.

The chain was long and heavy with a medallion attached to the bottom of it. The chain was covered in blood, but it wasn't hard to make out the medallion. The medallion was actually a square name plate with the word "SWAG" encrusted in diamonds in the center. I could feel my blood begin to boil. My worry suddenly turned into anger.

"Swag did this!"

"Who?" Terence replied.

"Abony's no good, drug dealing boyfriend! If my sperm donor did what he said he was going to do to Swag. I bet Swag did this in retaliation."

"You talked to your father?" Terence looked surprise.

"I bet his chain was ripped off in the struggle."

I prayed this blood was his or at least partially his. I went into the kitchen and grabbed a plastic zip lock freezer bag. Terence looked at me like I was crazy.

"Nia, what are you doing? That's evidence!"

"Listen, I can't rely on the cops to find this fucker. I am going to have to find him myself."

If he has my sister and nephew, I would do any and everything in my power to get them back. I knew I had to get to Swag before the cops figured this out. Time was of the essence and by the time the cops actually arrived and found the right places to look, it may be too late for Abony and Andy. Terence reached over and grabbed my arm.

"Nia, listen to yourself. You're going to go hunt down some drug dealer? You're going to get yourself killed!

"I know, I'm probably not thinking rationally right now, but I have no other choice.

"Nia, let the cops do their job. They will find Abony and Andy."
I shot Terence a glare and he immediately let go of my arm. There was no way I was going to let anyone get in my way. I hate to admit it, but Terence was right, I would be killed out here on the streets looking for Abony and Andy. I am a freaking Advertising Executive, who was raised in the suburbs. What do I know about the streets? That's when an idea hit me. There is only one person I know that knows these streets and has the power to not only find Abony and Andy, but has the power to actually get them back safely. I winced at the thought, but I knew I needed his help.

"Terence, I have to find my father."

CHAPTER 10: JAKE WRIGHT'S DAUGHTER

"Your father?" Terence looked confused. He had never really heard me ever speak of my father. Even when we were planning the wedding, I told him I didn't want my no good sperm donor walking me down the aisle. I told him I would have Cliff give me away. He might be my younger brother, but Cliff was the only positive male figure in my life.

"Isn't your father like.."

"Like a scum bag? Yes. A big time drug dealer? Yes." I said cutting Terence off. I know if you play with snakes, you can't be surprised when you are bitten by one, but right now I needed a snake to catch another snake.

"Terence, I don't know where else to turn and my sperm donor is probably the only person that can help. To be honest, I hate asking him for anything, but I have to put my pride aside for Abony and Andy's sake."

Terence and I drove through the neighborhood looking for my sperm donors Mercedes. To be honest, I have no clue where he lives or where he operates his business, but I remember Cliff mentioning to me one time that our sperm donor employs quite a few young pharmacists in the neighborhood. The same neighborhood his daughter and his grandson have to live in. I guess there is no shame in some people's game when it comes to making money.

I asked Terence to pull his car up to a group of young boys standing on the corner under a stop sign. Terence looked over at me like I was crazy.

"You want me to pull my car over where?"

"Over there." I said pointing to the boys on the corner.

"Do you want to get us shot?"

"I guarantee you, those boys work for my father. Pull over so I can ask them some questions."

"You definitely have a death wish."

Terence reluctantly pulled the car over in front of the group of young boys. It kind of sucks because these same boys on any other block, could easily be college kids or young high school kids, just hanging out, but I knew they were dealing by the number of cars I watched pull up to them and then pull off. It looked like they were running a drive through at McDonalds. For the number of hours they were out there working that block, they were probably making less money an hour than an actual McDonalds employee.

Once Terence's car came to a stop, a young boy, no older than fifteen ran up to my window. He was wearing a pair of skinny jeans that were baggy around the waist and hanging off of his ass, an orange baseball cap tilted slightly to the right, revealing a head full of dreadlocks, and a tight white V-neck t-shirt that revealed his tattooed, skinny, muscular arms.

"What can I do you for, ma'am?"

I stared at the young boys teeth for a second before I responded. Every single tooth was covered in gold. This young boy should be in school somewhere. I thought to myself. I bet he's good at math, most of these kids out here are. They can count a transaction in a split second.

"I'm looking for somebody."

The young boy shot me a crazy look, like I was wasting his precious time.

"Look lady this ain't no information booth. You got cash. I got product. What up?"

"I'm looking for Jake Wright." I responded. The young boy almost jumped out of his vintage Jordan's.

"Ain't no Jake Wright here! Who are you Five-O?"
The young boy eye's widened when he heard me mention my sperm donor's name. He looked at Terence and then back at me. Then the young kid pulled a dark pistol from the waistband of his jeans.

"Listen, you two bess' be on yo' way if you know what's good for you. Sayin' that name round here isa' good way to get yo' ass shot."

"NIA, LET'S GO!" Terence yelled as he put the car in drive.
"My name is Nia Wright, Jake's daughter. Tell him I'm looking for him!" I yelled out of the window to the young boy as Terence sped off.

"Nia, you're crazy!! You're going to get us killed!"
Yeah, it's probably not a wise idea to drive up to a bunch of drug dealers and ask them questions about their boss. I had no other way of finding my sperm donor so I had no choice but to hit the streets

Despite Terence's protests, we let every street pharmacist in a 10 mile radius know that Jakes daughter was looking for him. The great thing about the streets, news travels fast. We were about to pull over to another block when a dark black Suburban with dark tinted windows pulled alongside our car. The back window of the Suburban lowered slowly, revealing a man with a grey receding hairline and a sinister smile.

"Word on the streets is some crazy woman claiming to be my daughter is lookin' for me."

It was my sperm donor. I breathed a sigh of relief. For a moment there, I expected it to be someone holding a shotgun out of the window at us.

"Oh, you're my daughter now? Last time we talked you didn't want anything to do with me."

I took a deep breath and swallowed my pride. I wanted to yell back "You no good, motherfucker! How dare you question my loyalty as a daughter! You're the one who ran out on us! But, I didn't. I kept my composure. As much as I wanted to curse him out, I knew I needed him. Abony and Andy needed him.

"Listen, I'm not here to ask you to go the Father/Daughter dance. I got over that shit years ago. I'm here because Abony needs you!"
My sperm donor smiled and rubbed his chin.

"Man, you are feisty, just like yo' mama' and no nonsense, like yo' daddy. I love it! You sure you don't want to quit that important job of yours and come work for me? You and I would run this city."

The thought of working with this man made me sick to my stomach. I kept a fake smile on my face and refused to respond.

"So, what's up with my baby girl?"
I reached on the car floor and grabbed the plastic bag holding Swags bloody chain and threw it into my sperm donors open window.

"What the fuck is this?" He responded.
"That's Swags chain, and that might be Abony's blood all over it."

I hated to be blunt, however sometimes you have to be with people like him. He examined the bag. With each turn of the bag, I could see the anger rising in my sperm donor's face.

"What the fuck you mean, this is Abony's blood?"

"I saw this chain sitting in a pool of blood in Abony's apartment about 20 minutes ago. Abony and Andy were nowhere to be found. I think Swag has them."

I could see the wheels turning in my sperm donor's head. He took a deep breath and gathered his composure.

"Sweetheart, are you sure this is Abony's blood?"
He hadn't called me sweetheart in years. I was immediately taken back to being a three year old again, standing in front of my father, telling him about how Shanice Myers the bully who took my Cabbage Patch kid from me on the playground. I needed his help then and I need his help now.

"I knew I shouldn't have left his ass breathing." My sperm donor mumbled under his breath. He motioned to the driver in the front seat, a massive mountain of a man with a thick neck.

"Take me to Swag's crib. We will finish were we left off. I guess that
mother fucker doesn't learn not to fuck with my baby!"
The thick necked driver put the car in drive and began slowly rolling down the street, without a second thought I jumped out of Terence's car and ran over the passenger side door of my sperm donor's Suburban.

"Nia, what are you doing?"
"I'm going with you!"

"Sweetheart, this is a man's job. I will take care of it. You stay here with yo' little doctor boyfriend. If that punk ass Swag has Abony I will bring her back, safe and sound. Trust me."
Before my sperm donor could protest, I grabbed the door handle and opened the back passenger side door and sat in the seat right next to him. I was not taking no for an answer. He didn't have a choice.

"You don't have a choice. That's my baby sister."

"That's my girl. Tough as fuckin' nails. You can go but he ain't coming." He said, pointing towards Terence in front of my door. I didn't even notice Terence followed me out of the car.

"Nia, I can't let you go by yourself. I'm coming with you."

"Listen, cuz. Do you plan on marrying my daughter one day?"

Terence looked over at me. I looked back at him and smiled.

"Yes, that's my intention!"

"You're some famous surgeon, right?"

"Yeah, I guess you can say that."

"Then you don't want any part of this. The shit we are going to do to that fucking rat would land you behind bars for the rest of your life. It's best you go home and read some of your medical books. Nia, is my baby girl. I will bring her home safe. I promise."

Terence was determined not to let me leave without him. I reached my hand out of the car window and grabbed Terence's hand. I promised him I would be safe and I promised I would return with Abony. I told him I loved him as the car started to pull away. Our grip loosened as the car sped up. I turned around and looked out of the back window of the Suburban. Terence was standing in the middle of street with both hands on his head as we drove away.

"That boy loves you, huh?" My donor asked.

"Yes he does." I replied.

CHAPTER 11: BANG

The car ride to Swag's apartment was awkwardly quiet. What do you say to a man who gave life to you, but hasn't spoken more than ten words to you in the last thirty some odd years? I stared out the car window and tried my best to stay positive. I know this story can only end in two scenarios: The best case scenario, is finding Abony bruised, yet safe. And the seconds scenario? Let's not even go there. I tried everything in my minds power to avoid thinking about the worst case scenario.

"You know I'm very proud of you?" My sperm donor said breaking the car's awkward silence. I looked over at him like he was crazy. I'm grateful for his compliment, but where in the world did that come from?

"Look, you don't have to be nice. Let's go rescue Abony and then after that we can go back to our normal lives." I responded. My sperm donor rolled his eyes and then smiled.

"Yo' you got that Wright blood in you, girl. You're a fighter to the end. I was serious when I said it. I'm proud of you. You've done excellent with yo' life."

How do you respond to something like this? I wanted to be civilized and say thank you for the compliment, but maybe he was right about my Wright blood, because I was not going to let him off the hook for walking out on us.

"What do you care? I'm a grown woman, now. You were never there for us, so you can go somewhere else with that!"

"Nia, I was there."

"You were what? I can't believe you're saying you were there for us!" I watched my sperm donor adjust himself in his seat and lean in closer to me. I must have touched a nerve, I could see it all over his face. He gathered his thoughts before he spoke.

"Nia, I made some crazy sacrifices to make sure you live the life you live. I'm a piece of shit! I aint' denying that! That's why I left. I've made some shitty life choices and I'm paying for them, but I didn't want you and your brother and sister to be influenced by my bullshit lifestyle. I don't know how to fix myself. I'm about this street life, so I did what I know best. I removed myself from your lives. I was out. You guys are better because I wasn't there. Believe me…I would have fucked it up.

As God as my witness, I was there for every one of your graduations-from kindergarten, high school and college. I sat in the back row so you wouldn't know and bounced once I saw you get that paper.

I sat outside of every birthday party from Chucky cheese to your sweet sixteen at the Fox and I made sure I got you a gift for every birthday. I didn't miss a single one! I made your momma keep it a secret, though. It was a price I had to pay and I know you hate me cuz' of it, but I would do it again if it meant you would live a good life."

My sperm donor's revelation was shocking. I felt like someone had just removed a veil from over my head and I was seeing the world through new eyes. Was he telling the truth or was this one of his hustles? The Wright's are infamous hustlers. I looked into his eyes to see if he was telling the truth.

"Why are you running game on me? You don't have to, I'm ok with our relationship."

He seemed to take offense to my accusation. I could see his fists clinch and his jaw tighten.

"Nia, I've been accused of being a lot of things, but I aint' no liar. I was there. I care about you guys. Let me ask you a question; how much was your tuition for school? Your four years at Howard cost over ninety gee's' and your two years at Harvard Business school cost well over a hundred grand. I know this because I paid for it cash. I put money in a college trust fund for you on your sixteenth birthday."

My jaw dropped. How in the world did he know how much my tuition cost? My mother told me she took out a loan to pay for my school, and to not worry about paying her back. All this time she's covering up for him?

"You paid for my college with drug money?"
"Damn, I just can't win with you can I?" He responded.

"I don't want anything to do with your dirty money!"
"Nia, that money's clean. I would never do that."

"I wasn't born yesterday. I will give it all back to you, every penny!" I wanted nothing to do with his dirty drug business and I don't know where I was going to get the money to pay him back, but I did know I didn't want to owe him anything.

My sperm donor was starting to get pissed. I know he meant well and was genuinely concerned about how I grew up, but his mentality is jaded.

"Nia, I hate to sound like some old mafia movie, but I've been spending the last ten years trying to get my business 100% legitimate. I have investments all over Georgia. I got partial ownership in laundromats, restaurants, car dealerships… You name it and I got a cut in it. My biggest dream is to open a bordering school for young girls. They can live on campus and go to school, or whatever. I plan to hire some of the best teachers in the world. It's kind of my way of giving back for the stupid shit I've done in life. I want to leave this world in a better place, when I go. I was going to surprise you and leave it in your name, so you can run it. You know, use your Ivy league education to help the hood."

"Are you serious? Are you really trying to open a school?"

My father looked up to his driver Lucas in the front seat.

"Hey Lucas, am I lying?"

Lucas turned his giant head to the side."

"No sir, Mr. Wright. He bought the deed for acres of land a month ago."

I was speechless. I spent years hating this man and all this time he was there and he was planning for my future.

"You're going to give the school to me?"

"That's right, sweetheart. It will be yours. We break ground next fall."

Without realizing what I was doing, I leaned over in my seat and gave my father a hug. He hugged me back. His hug was tight. It felt like he was releasing years of guilt with his embrace. I felt the same way. I can't say I fully forgive him for not being there but now I can understand why he did it.

Lucas parked the Suburban in front of Swag's rundown apartment complex. I knew Swag was home because I could see his god awful Lexus parked out front. I fought every instinct in my body to be reckless. I wanted to run up the stairs and beat the shit out of that fucking coward. *If he hurt Abony, he was going to pay!*

"Nia, we gonna' run up in dude's apartment. You can come up, but I want you to stay behind us. OK?" "Ok." I agreed halfheartedly. I really had no idea how I would react once I saw Swag's face.

I got out of the car and followed Lucas and my father up the flight of stairs to Swag's apartment on the second floor. It wasn't hard to figure out which apartment door was his. The words "SWAG TIME" spray painted in bright colors across the front of the door was a dead giveaway.

What a clown! I thought to myself. *What kind of drug dealer writes their name on their front door?*

"Excuse me miss Wright." Lucas said politely as he instructed me to back away from Swag's front door. Lucas was born in Italy, but grew up in Brooklyn. He was a massive man. He looked like an ex-football player turned hitman. His shoulders were broad, his head unusually large and his arms and legs were the size of tree trunks. Lucas lifted his giant leg and with one massive blow, kicked in Swag's door. The impact sent the door crashing to the floor and before I knew what was going on, Lucas and my father were rushing into Swag's apartment.

Frightened, Swag jumped up from the couch and grabbed a shiny black hand gun sitting on the coffee table amongst a stack of weed and cash. There was a young topless girl sitting next to Swag on the living room sofa. Without hesitation, Swag grabbed the girl and wrapped his left arm around her neck, using her as his human shield. Lucas removed a shiny silver gun from his waistband and in one motion fired a shot at Swag.

BANG!

The shot rang loud in the apartment building. The bullet hit Swag in his right shoulder, knocking him to the floor and sending his hand gun flying across the room. Now free from Swag's grip, the young girl ran past us and out the front door screaming, her tiny breasts and waist covered in Swags blood. Lucas ran over to Swag and placed his giant foot over Swag's bullet wound.

"Where the fuck is Abony and my grandson?" My father asked as he stood beside Lucas.

"I don't know! I don't know! I swear!" Swag said as tears ran down his cheeks. My father removed the plastic bag containing Swag's bloody chain from his jacket pocket and threw it down on Swag's chest.

"Does this fucking bag jog your memory?"
Swag looked down at the bag nervously. His eyes rolled to the back of his head when he saw the bloody name plate with his street name on it.

"It wasn't me, man! I swear! I found her like that!"
"Found her like that? Found her like what? Where is my sister?" I screamed at Swag. My father turned to me and gave me the "Let me handle this look." I bit my tongue so my father could do his thing. My patience was low. Swag had about three seconds to fess up, before I jumped on him.

"Where the fuck is she? I'm not going to ask again!" My father demanded. Swag's eyes peered nervously at the door leading to the back bedroom and then back to my father's angry gaze.

"Don't kill me, please don't kill me! I love Abony!" Swag pleaded. My father walked over to the back bedroom door and pushed it open.

"I swear to all things good! If you harmed a hair on my baby girl's head. You're going to pay with your life!" My father said before he entered the bedroom. I ran behind him, hoping for the best. *Abony is probably in the back bedroom, ashamed because she went back to that fucking loser, Swag. All I care is that she's safe.* I said to myself as I took a deep breath. This whole crazy day would finally be over. We can bring Abony home.

When I walked into the bedroom I could see what looked like Abony sitting in a rocking chair facing an open window. Her back was to us, so it was hard to tell if it was really her. As I got a little closer, I could see it was Abony. My heart was beating heavy in my chest with each step I took. I could see Abony's curly head of hair slumped slightly over to the side. My brisk walk turned into a run as I sprinted past my father who stood motionless with his gun by his side. "ABONY!" I yelled as I made it to the edge of my sister's rocking chair.

My heart fell down to my knees as I turned and looked at Abony. She lay slumped over in the chair, her clothes bloodied and her bruised eyes closed. The sun peered through the window, illuminating my sisters face. She looked like an angel. For the first time in a long time, she looked peaceful.

"Oh, no Abony!" I leaned in and held my sister in my arms. Her body was stiff and unresponsive. I tried shaking her but she wouldn't wake up. "Abony! Abony!" I cried.

Swag came running into the room with Lucas in tow. Swag ran past my motionless father and over to me and Abony.

"Abony, baby! I'm so sorry! I'm so sorry!" Swag confessed as he hugged both me and Abony!

"GET THE FUCK OFF OF US!" I screamed as I pushed Swag away. Swag fell to the floor with Abony falling right beside him. Tears filled my eyes as I caught a glimpse of Abony's bare waist. She had been stabbed right near her belly button. I screamed bloody murder as I jumped on Swag. I began pounding my fists into his face. Blood sprayed everywhere as Swags jaw turned tender from my blows. My father and Lucas ran up behind me and grabbed me, removing me from Swag and my rampage. I laid on the hardwood floor crying for my sister. All was lost. Abony was gone. I looked up at my father. His eyes were full of tears.

"You're going to pay for this!" He said with the gun pointed at Swag's head. "It wasn't me, Mr. Wright, I swear! Abony called me and said she needed a ride to bring Andy home. So I drove by her crib! I swear on my momma's soul!" Swag pleaded.

"That's bullshit! You killed my baby!" My father said as he leaned in closer for the kill.

"No, Mr. Wright! I love Abony! I would never do anything like this to her! It was that Preacher man!" Swag professed. My father loosened his grip on his gun as I watched the wrinkles on his forehead disappear.

"What preacher man?" My father said calmly.

"When I was heading into Abony's apartment. Andy was walking out with that famous preacher dude that's always on T.V. You know the one who freed them hostages. I didn't think nothing of it at first, but when I got inside. That's when I found Abony on the floor. That fucker must have stabbed her. I didn't know what to do, so I brought her here."

"Why didn't you bring her to the hospital, you fucking idiot?" I yelled at Swag.

"I got warrant's, yo'! They would have asked questions. I can't have that! I ain't going back to the bing." I looked over at my father. His stoic face was now gone, in its place was the look of a man who just had his heart ripped out.

"Was Abony alive when you got there?" My father asked Swag. Swag paused and looked over at Abony.

"Was she fucking alive? I am not going to ask you again!"

"Yeah…." Swag mumbled. He knew this was not the answer to tell the man who held his life in his hands.

My father looked over at me and with a slight nod of his head commanded me to leave the room.

"I'm not leaving!"

"Baby girl, I am not asking, I'm telling you. This right here is not for you." My father replied. Even though I wanted to see Swag dead, my father was right. This was not for me. I bent down on my knees, kissed Abony on the cheek, took a deep breath, closed my eyes and walked out of the bedroom.

BANG! BANG! BANG!

The gunshots sent chills up my spine as I peered out of Swags living room window down at the street below. The people on the street were unfazed by the sound of gunshots. They were as common as birds chirping and police sirens in this hood. The kids continued their basketball game in the park across the street, dope boys kept dealing, young girls continued playing on the stoop and the zombie dope heads continued their saunter up the block.

A few moments later, Lucas came walking out of the bedroom with Abony in his arms, her body wrapped in a bedsheet. I began crying uncontrollably. *Damn, Abony!*

"Let's get out of here, baby."

My father grabbed my shoulder and walked me down the flight of stairs and out to the front of Swag's apartment building.

"Do you think he was telling the truth?" I asked my father between my tears.

"Yeah, he was telling a truth. The eyes never lie." My father answered.

"I didn't want this life for you guys. This shit right here, is my fault. Abony paid for my sins. I will never live that down, Nia. I'm sorry."
If this was three hours ago, I would have told my father that it was indeed his fault. But that is too much of a burden to put on anyone's heart. We are all human and we make mistakes.

"Dad, Abony is an adult and she chose this life. Right now, all we can do in her memory is find Andy."

"You're right. We have to find my grandson. Do you know who this preacher man is?"

"Yes, I think I do." I said as we watched Lucas attempt to put Abony's body in the back of the Suburban. *At this point, I wish I was dead.*

BANG! a gun shot rang out on the street. A bullet struck Lucas in the neck. I watched as his body jumped from the bullets impact. Blood spewed from Lucas's neck like a broken water pipe as Abony fell from his arms to the sidewalk below.

BANG! Another shot rang out, this time hitting Lucas in the chest, knocking his massive body to the ground. I looked up to see where the gunshots were coming from. That's when I saw a man dressed in black standing behind the Suburban. I squinted my eyes to get a better look. It was a face I recognized and hoped I would never see again. The man had a pale face full of freckles. He lifted his gun, this time pointing it at me.

"What the fuck!" My father yelled as he jumped in between the freckled killer's gun and me. **BANG!!! BANG!!!** The gun rang, as the bullets made impact with my father's chest.

"DAD!!!" I screamed as my father fell to the ground. I looked down in horror as his legs twitched uncontrollably. The small red dots on his chest began to expand rapidly, staining his Gucci t-shirt with blood.

The freckled killer smiled, savoring the moment. He was about to fire down on my father again when he got a glimpse of the silver pistol I pulled out of my waist band and pointed at him.

"Oh, I see you brought protection this time. Hahaha… Do you know how to use that thing? The freckled killer joked as he stepped towards me. My hand shook uncontrollably. *Shoot him Nia, shoot him! Just point at your target and squeeze!* Marco's voice echoed in my head. As much as I wanted to shoot, I just couldn't. The freckled killer grabbed the muzzle of the gun with no fear of me firing.

"Just as I figured, all talk and no balls!" He said while removing the gun from my grip. The cockiness in his voiced triggered the animal in me. You should have seen his eyes when I jumped up and wrapped my hands around his throat. His eyes opened wide. He was not expecting my attack. With all of my power and all of my might, I tried to squeeze the life out of this freckled bastard. He was going to pay. He was fucking with the wrong one.

As hard as I squeezed, the freckled killer was just too strong for me. Still holding the gun in his left hand, he used his right hand to remove my hands from around his throat. We wrestled around on the ground as a crowd began to gather around us. The freckled killers gunshots must have finally excited the neighborhood. It didn't matter though, the crowd just sat by and watched as the freckled killer hit me in the head with the butt of his gun. I rolled over on the ground. The pain in my head was intense. I felt nauseous as my vision began to blur. I looked over at my father who lay next to me with blood gurgling in his throat as he attempted to reach for his gun. He was dying.

The freckled killer bent down and whispered in my ear before scooping me up. "I love the hunt, you cunt! I am going to love opening you up with my knife!"

I screamed for help as the crowd stood by and watched. I looked on as people held up their camera phones recording the entire fight. I could only imagine this video being played on Facebook or WorldStar a million times, for the pleasure of some disturbed individuals. I stopped kicking and screaming as the freckled killer carried me over to his car. I could have continued fighting. But why? At this point I didn't care if I lived or died. Abony was gone and my father was dying.

The freckled killer popped open the trunk of his car and threw me in. He looked down at me and smiled as he closed the trunk of his car. *Damn, Nia. You're going to die!*

CHAPTER 12: INTRUDER ALERT!

I lay in the trunk of the freckled killer's car overwhelmed by the darkness. It felt like I was in a coffin. I lay there sad, depressed and defeated. Not because I was about to die. Right now, I could give a shit about life. I just lost everything! Poor Abony was gone. What else did I have to live for? I could feel the tears stream down my face as the image of her lying lifeless in her chair, tortured my mind.

Oh god, Abony, I'm so sorry! I should have been there for you! I'm your big sister. I should have been there to protect you!"

And my poor mom… *Oh, god, mom!* This is going to absolutely kill her! Abony was always momma's baby and she spoiled Abony rotten. My mother would always deny it when Cliff and I called her out on it.

"She's not my favorite. All of you are my favorite. Abony just needs a little extra attention, that's all." My mother would always say.

 Growing up, Abony was always attached to my mother's hip. All she had to do was whimper and my mother would come running to her aid. Now Abony is gone and my mother will never see her again. The image of mom dressed in her black dress standing above Abony's grave sent unnerving chills up my spine. It was like someone just stuck their hand in my body and ripped out my soul. Life was a black hole. No reason to live. Fuck life!

To make matters worse. I found my father today and I most likely lost my father today. Can you say bitter sweet? I want to cry for him, but I cant. It's not that I don't love him. It's the fact that I didn't really know him. He saved my life by sacrificing his. Those are the actions of someone who loves you. The actions of a father, not the actions of a sperm donor. If it weren't for him, those bullets would have been in my body. I guess my father wasn't the bad guy I imagined him to be. He loved me and had been paving a way for my future ever since the day I was born.

A small tinge of hope was beginning to bloom inside my garden of pain. *I have to find a way to get out of here!* If not, my father's sacrifice would have been in vane and my mother would end up burying two daughters. I can't put that burden on her. This would be my inspiration to live. If not for me, then it would be for my mother, my father, Abony and Andy.

Oh my god, I forgot about Andy!!! As if life was not hard enough for him. Now, he's going to have to grow up without a mother! Did he really leave with Reverend Sycamore? Did Reverend Sycamore really kill my sister? My father believed Swag was telling the truth and I do too. They say vengeance is a dish best served cold. If that Rev is my sisters murderer and my nephews kidnapper, he is going to get a frozen dish of bullets. But, why would he do this?

Oh shit wait! A thought just occurred to me. Is Reverend Sycamore Andy's father? Is that why Abony was keeping Andy's fathers identity a secret? Was Abony threatening to tell the world the truth? Was she going to tell the Rev's wife? Mr. Perfect preacher boy's world would be rocked by this scandal.

I have to get out of this trunk! I have to find Andy!

BUZZZZZZZZ……BUZZZZZZZ……BUZZZZZZZZ

A buzzing sound jolted me back to reality as it echoed through the trunk of the car. At first I thought I was feeling the bumps in the road but I quickly realized it wasn't rough road I was feeling, it was my cellphone buzzing in the back pocket of my jeans. *The freckled killer forget to check my pockets for my phone!! Oh goodness, this may just be my ticket out of this trunk!*

The trunk of the car was cramped and dark. Beyond the occasionally illumination from the brake light, I couldn't see a damn thing. I rolled over on my side and made an attempt to grab my phone. It was a struggle at first, but I was able to get it out of my back pocket. The light from the face of the phone lit up the trunk like a Christmas tree. *Thank you lord!*

I had a missed call from Marco. *Oh, thank God for Marco! I have to call him back and let him know what's going on. Oh, God I hope he can get here in enough time!* I was about to hit redial when the phone began buzzing again. This time, I had two incoming calls. One from Marco and the other from Terence.

Shit, Terence! I forgot all about Terence! He must be worried sick. The last time he saw me I was rushing away with my father off to save Abony. I looked down at the phone. *What call do I accept? Terence or Marco?* I had no time to play around. I love Terrence but he can't help me right now. Only Marco could. *I'll call Terence back after I take Marco's call.* I struggled for a moment as my fingers shook above the screen of my phone.

"Hello!" I whispered. I didn't want the freckled killer to hear me.

"Nia?" Marco replied. His voice was music to my ears.

"Marco, thank God it's you."

"Nia, are you ok? Where are you?"

"No, I'm in a trunk!"

"A trunk?" Marco sounded surprised.

"I was kidnapped! Marco, he's going to kill me!"

"Shit! Well stay on the line. Sarge is trying to track your coordinates."

"Oh god Marco, please hurry!" I looked down at the phone. My hands were shaking nervously, as the phone illuminated the dark trunk. The battery was at 5%. It's going to die soon. So, I prayed it would last long enough for Sarge to track where the freckled killer was taking me."

"What about your sister. Is she ok?" Marco said calmly.

"Marco she's…" I couldn't even say the words. The more I tried, the harder I cried. I couldn't stop my lips from quivering.

"Marco, she's dead!"

"Oh goodness Nia, I'm so sorry. I promise I will do everything in my power to get to you. We're getting close."

The car came to a sudden stop. My body rolled and I bumped against the back of the trunk.

"What was that?"

"I think we've stopped." I whispered back.

I could hear the car door close from outside of the trunk and the sounds of footsteps as they got close to the trunk.

"Oh goodness Marco, he's coming!"

"Nia, It's going to be alright. I promise."

This was it. No matter how fast they tracked me, Marco and Sarge would not be here in enough time to rescue me. I had nowhere to go this time. The freckled killer was going to kill me!

"Marco, I'm scared. You won't make it in enough time!"

"Nia, I need you to relax. If he was going to kill you he would have already done it. They want the microchip. Do me a favor, hide the cellphone in the trunk. We will continue to track you. Nia, I promise I will be there as fast as I can." Marco said calmly.

"Ok, I will. I love you!" I blurted out.

There was a pause on the other end of the phone. *Oh my goodness, did I just say that?* I took the phone away from my ear before Marco could respond. *He must think I'm crazy.* I took a deep breath and searched frantically around the trunk for somewhere to hide my phone. I found a toolbox in the back of the trunk or I should say it felt like a toolbox in the dark. I opened the small toolbox and placed the phone inside just as the freckled killer opened the trunk's door. The sunlight from outside of the car was blinding.

"Now don't try anything fucking stupid." The freckled killer said to me as he stared down at me in the trunk. He looked like a hungry fox staring into a hen house from behind a chain linked fence. The freckled killer wanted blood. I could see it in his eyes, but something was holding him back.

"Is she in there?" A male voice said from outside of the car. I recognized the voice. It was Bo Vista.

"Yes sir. I told you I would find her."

Bo Vista came out of the shadows and stood in front of the trunk. I looked up at him, but he refused to look back. He stood there sipping his cup of coffee, with his hipster glasses, polo shirt and his perfectly cut blond hair. He was smug and comfortable, while I lay in this stupid trunk.

"IS THIS HOW YOU TREAT ONE OF YOUR EXECUTIVES?" I yelled out of the trunk.

"Nia, I'm sorry it has to be this way. Out of all the people in the world. That damn microchip ends up in your body. What are the odds?"

"Are you going to kill me?"

Bo closed his eyes and then turned his head.

"Nia, you know entirely too much."

"Bo, are you going to kill me? Answer the question!" I tried hard to make eye contact but Bo refused to look at me. I was hoping I could appeal to the Bo I knew for so many years.

"Take her out of that god-awful trunk." Bo ordered.

The freckled killer reached in the trunk and in one motion swooped me out of the trunk and on to his shoulders. *Hurry up, Marco!*

Once out of the trunk, I was able to get a good look at the surrounding area. *"Where in the hell, are we?"* I thought to myself. We were deep in the woods, somewhere. The trees were so large I could barely see the sky. There was a large barbed wired fence surrounding the place, with dozens of armed guards dressed in black, patrolling the area. It looked like some type of secret fortress hidden away from the rest of the world. I could scream for days out here and no one would ever hear me.

There were black military looking jeeps, four wheelers, motorcycles and helicopters perfectly lined up on the grounds as armed men dressed in black, tinkered with them. Bo had his own secret little army.

The freckled killer carried me to the entrance of a large stone building. The building was the size of a small hotel and stood out like a sore thumb amongst the trees of the dense forest. I watched as Bo saluted the two guards holding large machine guns at the fortress entrance. Bo placed his hand on a small glass window on the side of the door handle. An infrared light scanned Bo's palm.

"Welcome back, Mr. Vista." A female robotic voice said as the front door of the fortress opened.

"Thank you, Ripley." Bo replied.

"I see we have two guests, Mr. Vista. Should I have two rooms on the guest wing made available?"

"Oh no, Ripley. They are not here for leisure. Please prepare a room in the research lab, and please don't let Katy know the guests have arrived."

"Oh sorry, Mr. Vista. Katy programmed me to inform her when Nia Wright arrived on campus. She is fully aware our guest is here."

"Shit! Ok, thank you Ripley."

"You are welcome Mr. Vista. I also detected Ms. Wright arrived in the trunk of a car. Upon her departure should I plan for a vehicle with a large trunk to accommodate?"

"No Ripley. Please erase that footage from the security camera's memory."

"Footage has been erased." Ripley replied.

The interior of the fortress looked like a large research facility. I can only imagine the top secret crap Bo had going on in this place. The freckled killer carried me into a room labeled "RESEARCH ROOM 1" and placed me down on a cold hospital bed. Bo looked up into a security camera in the ceiling in the corner of the room and instructed Ripley to secure my bed. Electronic shackles lifted automatically from the sides and bottom of the bed securing my wrists and ankles. I tried to squirm and get away, but my efforts were useless.

"I'm sorry it has to be this way, Nia. I promise you, this won't be painful. Dr. Ling will give you an injection and you will slowly fall asleep.

You won't feel a thing."

"Please Bo, don't do this! It's me, Nia. You know, your fucking friend! I've sat in your living room and watched the Super Bowl with you. I was at your 10th wedding anniversary party last year, I helped Vista Visions become a multibillion dollar company. Bo you know me! You can't do this!"

I tried everything in my power to appeal to Bo. I had no clue what that injection Dr. Ling was going to give me will do to me. Was it anesthesia or was it poison?

"Nia, I'm sorry. I can't let that video see the light of day. It will destroy everything I've built."

I watched nervously as Dr. Ling, dressed in a white lab coat prepared the needle on a table by my bedside. Everything seemed so cold and impersonal. *I can't believe I'm going to die like this!* I closed my eyes and prayed this would be over quickly.

"What the fuck is going on in here?"
I opened my eyes and watched as Katy Vista stomped into the room.

"Katy, we're going to remove the chip from Nia." Bo replied.
"So why is he giving her a needle?" Katy stepped in front of Dr. Ling and snatched the needle from his gloved hand and smashed it down on the floor.

"After all this bitch has done to us! You're going to be gentle with her? I hired the best to find her and we are going to rip that chip out of her body and bury this bitch in the woods."

"But Katy, we don't have to kill her!"
"What, are you still in love with her?"

Still in love with me? What was Katy talking about? My relationship with Bo was always professional. Bo kind of had a crush on me, but that's all it was, a little harmless crush. Katy walked over to the bed and looked down at me.

"I know your little games. You walk around the office flaunting that big booty of yours in front of my Bo! He's so stupid! He fell in love with your slutty ass. That's the only reason you got a promotion."

Katy better be glad I was strapped to the bed because if I wasn't, I would have ripped her head off of her shoulders. Katy looked over to the freckled killer and commanded him to come to my bedside.

"Do you have your knife on you?"

"Yes Ma'am, I do." The freckled killer responded as he removed the knife from a sheath attached to his belt. It was the same knife he used to stab Terence. I could tell because it still had Terence's blood all over it. The asshole didn't even take the time to clean it. The freckled killer held the knife up like a trophy.

"I want to remove the chip from her lungs. There's no need for anesthesia." Bo ran over and grabbed the freckled killers arm.

"No, Katy!"

"Sit your ass down, Bo!" Katy commanded.

Katy grabbed Bo and pushed him out of the way. Bo stumbled a bit and then fell to the floor.

"You're the reason this video exists! You're the one who wanted us to get in bed with the fucking enemy!" Bo yelled from the lab floor.

"You enjoyed every minute of it!" Katy replied with a sinister smile.

"Looks like you're going to be a problem, Bo. Let me guess you don't want to see your little girlfriend get hurt?"

Katy instructed the freckled killer to hold Bo down and make him watch as she used the knife to remove the chip from my lungs. Katy brandished the knife as she leaned in. I could feel her hot breath on my face. I felt nauseous.

"Please Katy, don't do this!" Bo and I said in unison.
"It's too late now, you little slut!"

Katy took the knife and ripped it across my chest, tearing my shirt to shreds, like a wild jackal.

"UGHHHHHHHH…..!" I moaned. It was the most painful feeling in the world! I squirmed in the bed and tried to break free.

"Hold still!" Katy barked as she gripped the knife tighter. The pain intensified by a thousand as Katy pushed the knife slowly into my chest, right above my breast. She looked down at me, smiling. The sick, jealous bitch! I felt the knife scrape against my rib cage as she dug deeper.

"Noooooooo…..!" I moaned. My voice echoing in the room. I could see my blood squirt up all over Katy's face. The pain was unbearable. I was dying.

Katy kept fishing with her knife as she searched for my lungs. Everything began to blur and the room started to spin slowly. I was blacking out. I could see Bo on the other side of the room. He was staring at me, his eyes bloodshot.

"Help!" I mumbled as blood gurgled in my throat and mouth. I could hear faint gunshots and a commotion from outside of the room. Everything started fading to black, as blood oozed all over my chest. The last thing I heard before passing out was Ripley's voice over the loud speakers.

"Intruder alert….Intruder alert."

CHAPTER 13: SCANDALOUS

I opened my eyes slowly, hoping this was all some sort of a crazy dream. I imagined myself lying in bed next to Terence on a warm Saturday morning. I also imagined Terence leaning over and giving me a big hug as we would cuddle in bed all morning. Bliss!

I was jolted back to reality by the smell of rubbing alcohol, gauze, blood and a loud security siren. I opened my eyes and looked around the room. I could see armed security guards run by the research lab door, frantic, with their guns drawn.

"Intruder alert….Intruder alert….Intruder alert….Intruder alert."

Oh please let this be Marco and Sarge coming to rescue me!

If I am seeing all of this, this means I am still alive! And this also means Katy didn't kill me and thrown me in a ditch, like she promised.

"Ughhhhh!" The pain in my chest was absolutely excruciating! It felt like someone was stabbing me with a knife and then rubbing salt on it to add insult to injury. (Kinda' accurate in this case). The room began to spin as I lifted my head to see what was going on.

My entire body was covered in blood and there was a gaping wound the size of a quarter on the right side of my chest, just above my breast. It looked disgusting as jagged mounds of flesh protruded from the hole.

Nia, you're going to have to get up and get out of bed before you bleed to death!

My efforts were useless. I was still strapped to the freaking bed! I couldn't move no matter how hard I tried. I looked around the room, Katy and the freckled killer were gone. *Thank goodness!* They must have left the room to see what set off the intruder alarm. Off in the corner of the room, I could see Bo tied to a chair. He looked semiconscious as he sat there, slumped over in his seat. His face was beaten, bloody and bruised. I looked on in horror as his head slowly wobbled back and forth.

"Ughhhh!" Bo moaned in pain. He was trying to wiggle his left hand free, but couldn't because there was a knife slashed through it, fastening it to the handle of the chair. It was the freckled killer's knife. It had to be. It looked just like the one he used on Terence. *Fucking Katy!* She must've done this in retaliation to the fake love affair she imagined Bo and I held secretly behind her back.

Bo lifted his head slightly and looked up at me.

"Nia....are.... you ok?" Bo said as he struggled to speak.

"I have to get out of this bed or I'm going to bleed to death!"

"Katy..... got the chip....she didn't get....to finish the job."

Blood started trickling out of Bo's mouth as his eyes fluttered and his head bobbled back. It would only be a matter of seconds before he completely blacked out. I had to find a way to get free and Bo was my only hope.

"Bo, do you think you can get me free?"

"Katy.... is not... going to like.... that at all!"

"Bo, I need to stop this bleeding before I die."

"No...Katy...will kill me."

I went to my last resort, my last ditch effort to appeal to Bo. I don't like to lie when it comes to the matters of the heart, but I had to go there.

"Bo, I love you. I've always loved you. You have to get me out of this bed so we can be together."

Bo's little head popped up when he heard my profession of love. I could see what looked like a half smile on his face.

"RIPLEY!" Bo commanded.

"Yes Mr. Vista, how can I be of service?"

"Please… release."

Bo's chin fell to his chest before he could finish.

"Sorry Mr. Vista. I did not hear your command."

"Release me, Ripley!" I yelled at the speaker in the ceiling.

"Sorry, voice not authorized!" Ripley replied.

"He was just about to say release, Nia. So release me already!"

"Sorry voice not authorized! For unauthorized users, I can command a beverage or access to the restrooms. Would you like either?"

"No, I don't want access or a beverage, you bitch! Release me from this table!" I yelled. The pain in my chest intensified. Yelling was not helping my case.

"How rude of you! Vulgar language is unacceptable! Access denied!"

I looked over at Bo. His chin was still tucked into his chest and he looked like he was mumbling something.

"Bo, wake up! Tell Ripley to release me."

Bo forced his left eye open and turned his head in my direction.

"Release….Nia." Bo said with his last breath.

"Your wish is my command. Nia Wright has been released."

I could feel the automatic restraints release me from their grips. I struggled to sit up in bed. I had to take it slow. I was weak and losing a lot of blood.

I slid off of the hospital bed. "THUMP" was the sound my lifeless feet made when they hit the cold floor. I immediately fell to my knees and then I came crashing down on my face. It felt like my jaw shattered. The room began to blur as a ringing sound in my ears trickled through my brain. I laid there on the cold concrete floor trying to gather the strength to move.

C'mon Nia, you have to move! You have to get out of here before Katy and her freckled goon returns!

With every ounce of energy I could muster, I crawled over to a glass cabinet on the other side of the room. I used the left side of my body so my wound wouldn't touch the floor as I crawled. With all of the energy I could summon, I pulled myself up to my knees. "Jackpot!" I mumbled as I rifled through the middle drawer of the cabinet. I lucked out. The cabinet held all types of medical supplies. I grabbed a giant medical bandage and a roll of medical tape. I pulled my shredded shirt to the side, exposing my wound to the cold air in the lab. "Ughhh" The cold felt like it was going through my bones. I saw bright red and stars as I placed the bandage over the jagged hole in my chest. "UGHHH!" The pain was unbelievable.

I fell on my back and gritted my teeth as the wringing sound in my head continued its concerto. I closed my eyes and used my left hand to search for the medical tape that just fell out of it. "There it is!"

I grabbed the roll of medical tape and took a deep breath before placing it over the bandage. My patch job was crappy and I would never be confused for a nurse, but it worked. The bleeding began to slow as the bandage sopped up the oozing blood. *Ok Nia, time to get up!*

I took a few deep breaths and attempted to get back up on my feet. Dumb move! My legs were about as strong as noodles, so I dragged my body to the exit. I pushed open the door with my head and pulled my body through it and out into the hallway.

The hallway was surprisingly empty. I expected it to be filled with security guards but there was no one in sight. They must be out dealing with "the intruder."

I looked up and saw a room right across from me with a sign on the outside of the door that read: "Audio Visual Lab." The door was slightly open and I could hear a faint, yet consistent noise coming from the room. I could barely make out the sound over Ripley's intruder alerts emanating from the speakers in the hallway. It sounded like a video playing in the room. I decided I would crawl into the Audio Visual Lab and muster up my energy, plus I have to admit the sound coming from the room sparked my curiosity.

Once inside the room, I found a computer chair in front of a wall full of computer monitors. I was able to grab the chair and pull myself up. I stood on my feet momentarily and then my body's momentum and my weak noodle legs forced me down to the chair below. I took a deep breath as I stared at the monitors.

The monitor in the center was playing a grainy video of what looked like three people in a dark bedroom, while the other monitors stood blank. This was without a doubt the source of the noise I heard outside in the hallway. I looked down at the counter below the monitors, there was a small port that read "Microchip processing" attached to a bunch of audio video components. That's when it hit me… *This was THE video! The video that was once attached to my lungs. The video that Bo and Katy didn't want the world to see!*

The video was dim, but I could easily see faces and naked bodies lying on a lavish bed in an expensive looking bedroom. Bo was lying on his back with his arms propped behind his head, while a naked Katy lay over him on all fours with her face buried in his crotch. Behind Katy was a rather skinny man with an unusually hairy body. From behind, he held Katy's bottom tightly as he thrust in ecstasy. I couldn't make out his face at first, because the camera was too far away. *Who is this mysterious man they were sharing their bedroom with?* The camera zoomed in close to the mysterious man's face, as if responding to my inquiry. I gasped out loud. I wasn't expecting it to be him. I imagined the Vista's sharing their bedroom with some famous actor or politician. This was scandalous, earth shaking. Now I know why Katy and Bo were willing to kill to keep this video from surfacing. The Vista's were in bed with the most wanted man in the world. I thought this video would be bad, but not this bad.

The Vista's were having a threesome with Michael Asir Jacques, the leader of the M.A.I.O. terrorist group. The man responsible for bombing a soccer tournament in California in 2003 that killed over 3,000 people and the man who held Marco and the news reporters hostage in Khaberistan.

What in the world were the Vista's doing in bed with Michael Asir, the half French, half Khaberistanian bomber? Once the world found this out, Vista Visions reputation will be destroyed. Were Bo and Katy Vista partnering with Michael Asir Jacques?

Now that I think back, the security leaks at the bombing in California kinda' sorta' financially benefited Vista Vision's software, because Bo swooped in with his budding software company and promised the world a fix to all of its security breaches. Bo had been planning for a situation like this for years, then this opportunity fell right into his lap. It was perfect timing. *A little too perfect if you ask me!*

Chills ran up my spine when I thought of the implications. Was

Michael Asir Jacques working for the Vista's? Was the attack planned so Vista Visions Software could profit from this catastrophe?

Before the tragedy, Vista Visions was a small company with only one hundred customers. After the attacks they became one of the biggest companies on the planet. *Nia, it's your duty to make sure the world see's this video. No matter what it takes! I have to bring Vista Visions Software to justice!* I said to myself.

I looked around the console for a way to make a tape recording of the Vista's video. My word would not be enough. I would need physical evidence to make them pay for their crimes. I took a deep breath and put my hand over my bandage in an attempt to hold in my pain. I closed my eyes and mustered up some energy. I had to get this done.

I looked at the computer monitor below the television monitors and read the words **"MAKE DIGITAL COPY"** in bold letters on the right hand corner of the computer screen. I grabbed the fancy computer mouse on the desk and selected the "Make Digital Copy" option. A prompt appeared on the computer screen: **"PLEASE INSERT FLASH DRIVE OR DISK"**

As I worked, I could hear loud gunshots out in the hallway. They were a way's off in the distance, but too close for my comfort. I rifled through the drawers in the cabinet below the computer monitors. I had to find a flash drive or disk I could use to save this video before whomever was firing that gun decided to enter this room.

Jackpot! I found a drawer filled with Vista Visions Software flash drives. I removed one and placed it into the USB port in the computer. Within seconds, the computer screen read **"VIDEO SAVED TO DRIVE."**

Just as I was about to do my little victory dance. Katy and the freckled killer came barging into the room.

"GRAB THAT FUCKING VIDEO! YOU HAVE TO DESTROY IT, BEFORE HE GETS HERE!" Katy screamed at the freckled killer. Katy and the freckled killers backs were to me, so they had no idea there was a guest in the room. The freckled killer and Katy turned around simultaneously and saw me slumped over in the chair in front of the computer monitors.

"How in two fucks, did you get in here!?" Katy said as she stared back at me menacingly. It only took a fraction of a second for the math to compute in Katy's head. She looked down at the flash drive in my hand and commanded the freckled killer to take it from me.

"With pleasure!" The freckled killer responded as he ripped me from my chair and threw me to the floor. My bones made a loud cracking sound as my body hit the floor. Before I could react, we were interrupted by a loud gunshot. Simultaneously, we all looked towards the glass door at the entrance of the Audio Visual lab. One of the guards dressed in all black fell to the ground in the hallway right in front of the glass door. He laid there lifeless, his eyes glossy, as blood trickled from his mouth. From the shadows of the hallway emerged Marco. I took a deep breath as Marco stepped over the soldier and pushed the lab door open.

"MARCO!" I gasped as he walked through the door. Marco my knight in shining armor was here to save me. It couldn't have come at a better time. Marco raised his gun at the freckled killer.

"Get away from her!" He commanded.

The freckled killer grimaced before standing erect. Marco commanded him to drop the knife he was holding.

The freckled killer was quick with the knife. I didn't even see him remove it from his waistband. The freckled killer frowned like an infant forced to give away his bottle of milk. He let go of the knife and I watched it fall on the floor next to me.

The knife had not even settled on the floor when Katy grabbed Marco's arm. Surprised by the attack, Marco accidentally fired a shot into the ceiling as he wrestled with Katy for control of his gun. Seeing an open opportunity, the freckled killer ran over and took over the wrestling match by wrapping his arms around Marco's neck. Marco's eyes turned bloodshot red as he struggled to get free. Katy stood by and watched Marco's demise with a sort of demented, awkward pleasure.

After a little struggle, Marco was able to free himself from the freckled killer's choke hold. Marco and the killer stood toe to toe exchanging blows to each other's faces. One of Marco's shots knocked the freckled killer off balance and that's when Marco found his opportunity to strike. Marco picked up the wobbled freckled face killer and body slammed him on top of a desk. The freckled killer moaned loud as his body crumpled on top of the desk. He rolled off the desk and to the floor, slowly rising back on his feet. Without hesitation he jumped on Marco, pushing Marco into the computer monitors on the wall behind me.

The momentum caused Marco to drop his gun as he lay on the ground next to me. I stared at Marco's face. If I didn't know any better I would say he was smiling, enjoying the art of the battle.

"Marco, get up!" I mumbled.
The freckled killer ignored the gun and jumped on top of Marco. He placed his hands around Marco's throat and began choking him again.

Marco's eyes began to bulge and my heart dropped as Marco struggled for breath. I was not going to sit idle while the man I loved was being murdered right next to me.

I took the flash drive and put it in between my teeth as I got up to my feet. It took a power I didn't know I had in me, to get up. I jumped on the freckled killer's back and took my arms and wrapped them around his neck as he continued to choke Marco. With all of my might and power, I squeezed the crap out of the freckled fucks neck. He groaned. The pain was so intense, he had no other choice but to let go of Marco. The freckled killer stood up with me straddling his back, his arms flailed around in the air in attempt to get me off of him. I continued to squeeze as hard as I could. I could feel him weakening. The pain was too much for him. The freckled killer fell backwards with me underneath him.

The momentum and pain of this giant man falling on top of me, caused me to lose my grip around his neck. I lay on the ground with the freckled killer on top of me. I could feel him trying to get to his feet. He would get up and make me pay for choking him. I searched the floor around me for something I could grab that would knock out or slow down the freckled killer. That's when I saw his knife lying on the floor next to us. It was like poetic justice, the knife that he used to stab Terence was lying there waiting for me to use it.

I grabbed the knife and gripped it tightly in my hand. Without hesitation and in one mighty blow, I stuck the knife into the freckled killer's neck. Blood gushed everywhere as he moaned in pain. All I could think about was Abony, my father and Andy. My anger was fueled by their pain. I took the knife out of his neck and kept stabbing the freckled killer.

With each stab it felt like a slow release from my pain. I can't remember how many times I struck him, but I do know I didn't stop until his body went limp. I don't know what came over me. I just knew I didn't want this man to ever hurt anyone again.

I looked up from the bludgeoned body that lay on top of me. I caught a glimpse of Katy staring down at me. I could only imagine the thoughts going through her mind as I lay there covered in blood with the flash drive still tucked in between my teeth. I must have looked like a wild animal, after finishing off her prey. Katy brought it out of me and there was no way in the world she was going to make an attempt to get the flash drive out between my teeth without losing her life in the process.

I could see a mix of terror and anger in Katy's eyes as she stared down at me. She was not happy at all that I had the upper hand on her.

"This isn't over with!" Katy said right before she ran out of the lab door.

CHAPTER 14: TWO ENDLESS SOULS FINDING THEIR PLACE IN THE UNIVERSE TOGETHER

Marco pushed the freckled killers limp, bloody body off of me. Then he extended his hand and helped me to my feet. My legs may have been weak, but they were strong enough for me to wobble over to the door. I gazed out into the hallway. I was looking for Katy. With what little power I had, I wanted to chase after her and bring her ass to justice for what she did to me. Marco held on to me and convinced me that chasing Katy was a worthless cause. We had the video that will destroy their empire. That's all we needed. The court of public opinion will be her final judge. Marco looked down at the bloody makeshift bandage covering my chest. It was visible through the rips in my shirt.

"Oh God Nia, I'm so sorry. Look at what they did to you! I should have gotten here sooner!" Marco professed.

"It's not your fault. If it weren't for you, I would be dead. Marco, you're my hero. You saved me!" I replied. Marco looked up at me and smiled. I know this is not the time nor the place, but my heart melted. For a moment, I forgot about my pain.

"Do you mind if I take care of your wound? We have to stop the bleeding." Before I could answer, Marco dashed out of the room.

"Where are you going?" I yelled at him as he ran out.

"There is a medical room. I saw it on the way in. I will be right back." Marco yelled from the hall. I sat down on the chair took a deep breath and waited for Marco's return. My shirt was drenched in blood. I guess my little bandage job was not doing the trick. I looked over at the freckled killer who lay face down on the floor across from me. *Damn, Nia! How did you get caught up in this mess?*

Moments later Marco returned with a medical kit in his hands and some sort of blue medical scrub shirt. I struggled to lift my shirt over my head. Marco blushed and then rushed in to assist. He kept his eyes locked on mine. He was the perfect gentlemen. Never once looking down at my bare chest.

"Do you mind?" Marco said before addressing my bandage.

"Please." I responded. I anticipated some severe pain when Marco removed my bandage. Instead he lathered it with water and then removed the bandage slowly. This is not how I imagined my first shirtless encounter with Marco to be. Not even close. I clinched my teeth as Marco applied some stitch stickers over my wound. It hurts like hell, but I wasn't going to let Marco know. Within a matter of seconds my wound was closed.

"There you go. As good as new!" Marco said as he placed a large bandage over the stitches.

"Do you think you can walk?" Marco asked.

"Barely." My legs still felt like noodles.

"I got you. I'll be your legs." Marco said as he scooped me up and carried me in his arms. For the first time in a long time, I felt safe again.

"A girl can get used to this." I flirted.

"Don't get too use to it. You are going to have to carry me next. I'm not that heavy." Marco said with a chuckle. We both laughed as Marco carried me through the doors threshold. Marco had a calming way about him. If I could, I would stay in his arms forever. I looked up at him as he walked. His scruffy beard and unkempt hair made him look like a gladiator as he carried me through the halls of the fortress and out to the courtyard. I looked on in horror as we passed the bodies of dozens of dead or wounded soldiers laying on the ground beneath us. Marco had gone through hell on earth to save me and I was forever in his debt. He was my hero. After it was all said and done, he kept his promise. Marco kept me safe.

Above us, Sarge circled the courtyard with his helicopter. Dust flew everywhere as he landed the helicopter in the center of the courtyard. There would be no resistance, Marco took care of that. Marco put me down on my feet and helped me climb up into the helicopter.

"Hello, sweetheart! A lot's changed since our last helicopter ride, huh? I'm glad to see you're safe." Sarge said as he turned around and smiled. I gave him a big hug and then slid over to my seat.

As the helicopter took flight, I took joy in knowing that once we land I would be able to return to my normal life. As much as I loved being with Marco, I was ready to return to my simple life with Terence. I would do anything to get back to being Nia Wright. I lost Abony today, but it will not be in vain. I will hire the best private investigator money can buy to find my nephew Andy. If Reverend Sycamore is Andy's father and if he is my sisters murderer he is going to pay for it in ways he could never imagine. I know it won't be easy. The reverend is a very powerful man, but he will pay. I can promise you that!

I kept my eyes closed and listened to the light conversation between Marco and Sarge. They talked about their time in the military together and laughed about Marco's impending life as a civilian. We had flown for thirty peaceful minutes and all was good until their conversation was interrupted by a call on the helicopters radio.

"**Air Command to unknown helicopter. You are flying in restricted airspace I command you to land this copter, immediately.**"

Sarge turned his head and looked over at Marco.

"That's Garret in Air Command, remember he flew a few missions with us back in 2005? I've known this dude for years. I don't know why he is commanding me to land this copter."

Sarge grabbed the helicopters radio.

"Air command this is Sarge one. What's the problem? I fly this route all the time."

"**Unknown helicopter, ground your copter immediately or we will be forced to ground you, ourselves.**"

"Garret what's up? Why are you pretending like you don't know me? This is Sarge! I will be flying my helicopter past your base like I always do. I am not aggressive. Stand down!"

"**Sarge, we are under direct orders. Land your copter now! You are carrying a wanted fugitive, Marco Silver. He is wanted in the connection with the murder of Todd Malone.**"

"Garret your intel is incorrect. Please stand down."

I looked over at Marco. Todd Malone was his neighbor, the fitness freak that was sleeping with his wife.

"This has to be a joke. I don't even know a Todd Malone."

Marco looked confused.

"Marco, Todd is your next door neighbor." I replied.

I could see a look of recognition come over Marco's face. I didn't like the look I saw in his eye, though. Marco looked nervous. When he left me in the barn, did he go home and catch Sarah and Todd together? All kinds of crazy thoughts went through my head. Maybe Marco caught Todd getting freaky with Sarah and in a fit of jealous rage...... I tried to clear the thought from my mind. Marco wouldn't harm a hair on an innocent person. Todd was guilty of sleeping with Sarah, but he wasn't a physical threat to Marco. Marco wouldn't harm him.

"Look Sarge, we don't want you. Marco has to be brought in for his crime and the young lady on the copter with you, she is carrying a very important asset. Turn her over and Ms. Vista will spare you, Sarge."

I turned and looked at Marco. This was a set up. Katy was behind all of this. Marco said the Vista's reach went far. I shouldn't have been surprised.

Garret at Air Command ordered us to land in a patch of land in a clearing woods one kilometer away from where we were now. I looked off in the distance, on the ground below us. There was blue and red flashing lights. The police were waiting on the ground for us. This was all planned. Katy was going to make sure she got her grubby hands on the video before we had a chance to share it with the world and I guarantee you once she had it, Marco and I would not be found alive.

"I don't give a crap what you say! I'm not turning them over to you!" Sarge yelled into the microphone attached to his headset.

"So be it, good buddy. You have been warned" The commander said calmly. Within a matter of seconds a black helicopter hovered alongside our helicopter. I recognized the flying beast. It was one of the military copters from Bo and Kathy's little fortress.

"Oh God, Marco, Sarge look!" I said pointing at the black copter.

The helicopter was nothing like the helicopter we were flying in. It had two giant cannons under each side of its wings along with what looked like two long cannons at the front of the copter. Sarge and Marco turned their heads towards the copter. Sarge grimaced.

"Shit! We have to get out of here!"

The helicopter swooped down towards us as if it were toying with us. As it got closer I could see its pilot, dressed in a black helmet and dark sunglasses along with someone else sitting next to him.

"It can't be!" I said aloud.

"What?" Marco turned to me, confused.

"There!" I said pointing at the passenger sitting next to the pilot. It was Kathy Vista. I shouldn't have been surprised. Kathy looked pissed as she stared at me through the window. Her beady little blue eyes sent chills up my spine. I watched as Katy raised her arm and mouthed the word "FIRE!" Before we could react, Orange and red flames exploded from the long cannons at the front of their helicopter, sending a barrage of bullets in our direction. Sarge yanked on the helicopter's steering stick to avoid being struck. It would be too late. A barrage of bullets struck the side of our helicopter, sending us into a uncontrollable tail spin.

"Sarge, you have to control the copter!" Marco yelled.

"I'm tryin'....I'm tryin'" Sarge barked back.

Kathy had no mercy. They had us right where they wanted us. Like a cat toying with a trapped mouse. Marco and I looked on in horror as a giant rocket ripped from the cannon on the side of their helicopter. The rocket struck the back of our copter. "BOOOOOM!!"

The tail of our helicopter exploded into flames. The impact threw

Marco and I into the cockpit of the helicopter next to Sarge.

"Sarge!" Marco yelled as he shook his unconscious friend. Sarge had blood covering his face from the impact of his head smashing into the front windshield of the helicopter. Marco pulled his friend aside and tried to take control of the helicopter.

"Put on your seat belt! This is going to be a rough landing!" Marco said to me from the font of the helicopter. Before the words could leave his lips the right side of our helicopter exploded. Kathy and her copter were firing on us again. She was not going to stop until we were dead. Our helicopter was going down fast and the cockpit was full of flames. In one hand Marco gripped Sarge's jacket, preventing him from falling out the new hole on the side of our helicopter and in the other hand held onto the steering stick. There were giant flames covering Marco's hand and arm as he gripped the stick tightly. I closed my eyes and braced for impact as our helicopter was about to come crashing down into the swamp beneath us.

CHAPTER 15: SWAMP

BOOOOOOM!!

Mud and giant flaming pieces of the helicopter went everywhere as we made impact with the swamp. My body jolted hard. If it weren't for my seatbelt, I would have probably been flung clear across the pond! Everything went black. My ears were ringing uncontrollably. All I could taste was dirty dingy water as I struggled to hold my breath underneath the murky swamp. I searched frantically for the seatbelt release button.

I'm going to freaking drown, if I don't get out of this helicopter! It was too dark and we were sinking fast. *Where's the button? Where's the button? Oh God, I can't find the seatbelt button!*

I felt something grab ahold of my hand. It felt like another hand over mine. This mysterious hand began fumbling with my seatbelt. "CLICK" was the vibration I felt as the tension in my seatbelt loosened. I was free!! I could barely contain my breath as the hand grabbed a hold of mine and began pulling me out of the submerged helicopter.

"HHUUUUHH" I gasped for air, as I made it to the swamps surface. My lungs were on fire. I opened my eyes and wiped the mud from my face. I could see blue and red lights glowing off in the distance. Behind me, the tail of the copter poked out of the water. The rest of the swamp was engulfed in flames. *Damn, I must have nine lives! How did I survive that?*

I spotted a single police car parked several yards away from the front of the swamp. It's blue lights and siren where blaring in the night sky. I could hear a whizzing sound zipping past my head, like someone was flinging rocks at me, at a super-fast pace. *THOSE AREN'T ROCKS!!* I soon realized. They were bullets being fired from the military helicopter hovering above the swamp. They were making sure we were dead. I assume they couldn't see me through the smoke and flames because the bullets were sporadic, zipping in all different directions across the pond.

"MARCO! MARCO! MARCO!" I yelled into the night air. It had to be Marco who pulled me from the sinking helicopter, but where was he? Was he hit by one of the bullets?

"MARCO! MARCO! MARCO!" I yelled again.
From underneath the water, I felt something grab a hold of my leg. *What the hell is that?* I said to myself. Before I could react, a giant body surfaced out of the water next to me. The large man gasped for air. It was Marco! He was alive!

"SARGE! I CAN'T FIND SARGE!" Marco babbled to himself. I grabbed a hold of his shoulder and began to shake him.

"MARCO, WE HAVE TO GET OUT OF HERE!" It will only be a matter of time before we are struck by one of these bullets. Confused, Marco looked around us. The bright red and orange lights from the flames of our burned helicopter shadowed his face. Marco snapped back to reality.

"Nia, I have to find Sarge! He's still in the helicopter."

"MARCO NO! WE DON'T HAVE ENOUGH TIME!"
Before the words could even leave my lips, Marco had dipped back underneath the water. He was determined to find his old friend. I feared he was too late.

"DON'T YOU MOVE A MUSCLE! I WANT YOU TO PLACE YOUR HANDS ABOVE YOUR HEAD!" A voiced echoed from behind me. I turned around quickly. There was a young police officer standing at the edge of the pond. He looked like he was barely twenty years old. He was tall and rail thin. His uniform was way too big for him. He looked like a young child playing dress up. The young officers hands shook as he pointed his gun in my direction. I could see sweat dripping down the sides of his forehead as he barked orders at me.

"RAISE YOUR HANDS ABOVE YOUR HEAD!"
He commanded, nervously. I closed my eyes and took a deep breath as I struggled to stay afloat. The cop looked around frantically. He had to be the first officer on the scene. Off in the distance, I could hear the loud sirens and blue lights of another cruiser making its way to the swamp. I raised one hand in the air as I crawled out of the swap.

"Where is your soldier boy?" The young officer asked as his eyes scanned the pond behind me. "They say he killed somebody. Our orders are to shoot both of you on sight!" He said in a southern drawl.

"It's not true, I swear!"
The young officer looked me in the eye before speaking.

"I didn't take this job to shoot no woman. My momma raised me better than that. You and I are going to walk over to my cruiser and wait for my backup to arrive. Don't do anything stupid, ma'am."

For fear of being shot by this rookie, I did as I was told. There was no reason to make a fuss. If this officer had orders to shoot to kill, then I had no reason to argue with him. He was sparing my life. If he only knew, I was truly the one Kathy Vista wanted dead. I was the one with the video of her and Bo getting nasty with terrorists.

The young officer walked beside me with his gun drawn. He walked backwards the entire time with his eyes and gun focused on the swamp.

"I want you to get in the back seat and not say a word! You understand?" The officer said as he opened the back door of his cruiser.

The police car was ancient. It looked like it was driven out of a 1950's time warp. It smelled rank, like old sweaty balls and bullets.

"Yes, sir." I replied as I slid into the backseat of the old cruiser. The officer slammed the door shut and I immediately felt claustrophobic, like an animal locked in a cage. Time was of the essence, so I searched for a way to get out of the cruiser, just in case I needed a way to make an escape. I tugged on the door handles in the backseat but they would not budge. They were locked for obvious reasons. The cruiser was so old so there were no security bars separating the front and back seats, like you see in the movies. It was probably because this police car is ancient as hell. If I had to, I could slide over the front seat to make my escape and if the doors were locked, I could climb through the drivers side's open window.

I had a good view of the swamp through the front window of the cruiser. I watched the young officer standing in front of the water's edge with his gun drawn. He was waiting for Marco to break the surface of the water.

Oh God Marco, please swim to the other side of the pond!

The siren of another cruiser was close. I watched as it zoomed past me. The police cruiser parked right beside the young officer and I watched as a burly officer with a giant head and square jaw jumped out of the car. On the passenger side, his shapely partner jumped out as well. She had dark hair pinned in a tight bun, large hips and a tiny upper body. They bolted to the edge of the blazing swamp with their guns drawn. I could hear their conversation through the open window on the driver's side of the cruiser.

"Where are they?" The burley officer questioned the rookie.

"I haven't found the suspect yet. He's has to be still in the swamp. However, his accomplice is in the back of my cruiser!" The rookie said pointing his finger in my direction.

"The back of the cruiser? Our orders were to shoot to kill! Did you at least cuff her?" The female officer questioned. The rookie looked at her confused.

"Well, no ma'am. She's not who we are looking for. I believe the suspect is still in the water!"

"You fucking idiot!" The female officer responded. I watched in terror as her Burly partner grabbed ahold of the police radio on his shoulder. I could hear him say they found NIA. They both began walking in my direction. *FUCK!*

As if by divine intervention, Marco's head broke the surface of the water right in front of the Police officers. All three's attention left me and went right back to the swamp. Marco was holding a limp Sarge up against his chest. He looked up at the officers, confused.

They are going to shoot Marco! Just like Kathy Vista had instructed them to. I have to do something and I have to do it now!

My instincts kicked right in as I hopped over the front seat of the car. The keys were still in the ignition so I started the car and pressed my feet on the gas as hard as I could. "VROOOOOM" the engine of this old car was strong. I caught the officers totally off guard as my car barreled into theirs. SMAAAASH!!! The officers dove out of the way in fear for their lives.

I pushed the gas pedal to the floor, pushing their police cruiser into the swamp. Marco looked surprised to see me in the driver's seat of the police cruiser.

"GET IN!" I ordered Marco. Marco looked down at Sarge. His face was blue and lifeless. Marco took a deep breath as he laid his old buddy down on the ground and hopped into the passenger seat of the cruiser. I put the car in reverse and spun it around. A spray of bullets shattered the back window of the cruiser as I pressed my feet on the gas. We barreled down the road like Bonnie and Clyde.

CHAPTER 16: BONNIE AND CLYDE

I sped down the dark road with my foot pressed firmly against the gas pedal. We went for about twenty miles without seeing another car. I kept my eye on the rearview mirror, waiting to see the lights of a backup cruiser in hot pursuit. I looked over at Marco. His attention was elsewhere. Loosing Sarge, had to be weighing heavy on his mind. *I'm so sorry, Marco.*

I pulled the car over near a clearing in the woods.
"What's up, Nia? Why are you stopping?"
"We have to get out of this car. It's only a matter of time before they spot us on this road.

"Good idea. Turn off the lights. Let's go in a little deeper before we ditch this thing." Marco explained.

I pulled the car into the woods slowly. It was difficult to do with all of the trees in our way. Despite the trees, I was able to maneuver about a quarter mile before it was too dense to drive.

"This is perfect. We can go deeper on foot." Marco explained.
"Nia, grab the phone." Marco said, while pointing at the console of the car. Lucky us, the young police officer accidentally left his cellphone behind. I grabbed the phone quickly. *We can use this to upload the Vista's video to the internet.*

"Make sure you power it down. They can use it to track us."
I turned off the phone then slid out of the police car. Marco grabbed my hand and we limped as fast as we could deeper into the woods. I'm not going to lie, it was complete darkness and spooky as all hell out.

We walked through the woods for what felt like an hour before I had to stop and catch my breath. I looked over at Marco and he was doing the same. The days events had taken their toll on the both of us. Marco suggested we stop and build a camp for the night. I was about to agree, when I spotted something in the woods about one hundred yards away from where we stood. "Jackpot!"

In the corner of the woods was an old log cabin covered in wildlife. It looked abandoned and creepy. Like something from an old horror movie. Plants and trees made this cabin their home. It was the perfect camouflage from the rest of the world. We would have probably walked right past it if it weren't for the old rusty pickup truck parked by the side of the house. Marco walked up to the front door and tried to pry it open with a crowbar he found in the bed of the truck. I grabbed ahold of the door handle and we both pulled until the door almost ripped off its hinges.
Marco poked his head inside the door and then turned back and look at me.

"You go first, it looks scary as hell in there!" Marco joked.
"You must be out of your mind, if you think I'm going in their first!" I said while giving Marco a little shove. He tumbled forward and fell into the room. "Damn girl, it's like that? See if I ever rescue you again!" Marco joked.

I followed Marco into the old musty log cabin. He flipped the light switch near the living room door and in an instant the room came to life. *Thank goodness!* The house must have been running on solar power because I couldn't imagine there being electricity out in the middle of nowhere. The cabin wasn't half bad. It had a living room, kitchen, bedroom and bathroom. All of the essentials needed to recoup for the night.

Marco searched the cabin for the keys to the old red rusty truck on the side of the house, while I searched through the bedroom for clothes we could change in to. I had to get all of this mud, blood and filth off of me! I was about to rifle through the dresser when a picture on the bureau caught my attention. I picked it up and wiped off the dust and cobwebs.

It was a picture of a man and a woman. I would guess they were husband and wife and probably in their late thirties. The man wore a flannel shirt and a raggedy baseball cap. He had a big "Kool aid" smile on his face as he held his rifle by his side with great pride. Standing next to him was a woman wearing an identical flannel shirt. She didn't look as happy as her bearded husband. The frown on her face was a dead giveaway. The poor lady looked defeated. I could imagine she was tired of living out in the middle of nowhere. Why on God's green earth would they decide to make this place their home? I imagined them being two Yuppies who got bored with the hum drum of corporate life and decided to turn "earthy crunchy" and give away all of their earthly possessions to live off the land.

I put the photo down so I could rifle through the dresser. "Bingo!" I found a drawer full of clothing. The couple must have left them behind. I grabbed a pair of flannel pajama bottoms and a t-shirt. I also grabbed a pair of pants and a flannel shirt for Marco. I would assume he wanted to clean up as well.

I sat down on the dusty bed and pulled out the cellphone. *Ok Nia, you can do this!* I said to myself. It was time to let the world know about the Vistas. I wanted to upload the video before I hopped in the shower. I removed the flash drive from my pocket. It was soaking wet. *I hope it still works.* I attached the drive to the phone and in a matter of minutes I had the video uploaded onto Scandle.com's website.

I titled my little masterpiece - "VISTAS_SLEEPING WITH THE ENEMY." I sat back and watched as the video caught on like wild fire. It jumped from 1 view to 100 views in a matter of seconds. Within minutes, the video was shared over 300 times. It was going viral and fast. *Take that Katy Vista!*

I put the phone down and walked to the bathroom. I had to get this filth off of me. I walked over to the shower and prayed for water.

A woman lived in this house so there had to be running water.

Dirty brown water spewed out of the rusty shower head. I took a giant step backwards and was about to scream defeat when the water slowly turned into fresh clean warm water. I jumped into the shower and grabbed the bar of soap sitting in the soap dish.

Ughhh….the warm water felt great on my body. I didn't know how long it would last, so I savored the moment. I cleaned off all the dirt and blood from my body and hair and then hopped out of the shower saving some of the warm water for Marco. I found a first aid kit under the sink and replaced my bloody bandages. Thank goodness the bleeding stopped.

I grabbed the pajama bottoms and squeezed them over my hips. They were a little tight but I made them fit. I threw on the t-shirt and put my hair in a bun. I was a new girl. *Time to go see what Marco is up to.*

As I walked out of the bathroom, I noticed the entire house was dark with the exception of a glow coming from the front of the house. I walked slowly through the living room. The fire place was blazing. I caught a faint smell of pasta coming from the kitchen. *Marco, what are you up to?*

I was caught by surprise by what I saw in the kitchen. Marco was sitting at the kitchen table with two bowls of pasta in front of him. The kitchen was completely dark with the exception of the two candles Marco had lit in front of him. Goosebumps covered my arms and butterflies filled my belly. *Is this what I think it is? Is this a candlelit dinner!?* Marco stood up. He was wearing a raggedy old checkered apron.

"Beefaroni or Ravioli?" Marco said with a smile.

Oh God Nia, don't geek out in front of Marco. You can do this! I don't know who's more wet right now, me or my hair? Nia, get it together!

"Beefaroni of course. That's one of my favorites!" I said in my coolest voice. During my first year in college, I ate nothing but beefaroni. It was cheap and I loved to eat it. It was the perfect combination for a freshman on a budget.

I sat down at the table and Marco slid the plate over to me. Damn, he looked sexy as hell. This big muscular man serving me a hot bowl of beefaroni in a pink checkered apron. *It can't get any better than this!*

"Bon appetite." Marco said while rolling up his sleeves. He grabbed his plate of Ravioli and I watched him devour every bite.

"So Miss Nia, how does it feel to have surgery with a jagged knife, survive a helicopter crash and swim a swamp full of snakes, all for a bowl of my famous beefaroni?"

I laughed out loud. It was good to finally see Marco in good spirits.

"Is this how you treat all of your first dates? I hate to see what a woman has to go through for lobster and steak."

"Haha! I love simple meals. I'm a simple man. Now that I know your favorite meal, I bet you can't guess mine."

Before I realized what I was saying, I blurted out "Peanut butter and Jelly sandwiches." Marco looked at me like I was half crazy. *Damn, I wish I could take it back.* Marco had no clue I had been stalking his life while he was held hostage in a cave.

"How in the world did you guess that?"

I looked Marco in the eyes. There was no reason to beat around the bush we had been through hell and back again.

"Marco.. I kind of read the letters you wrote to Sarah and I kind of went on the dates, you set up for her. I know all about your mother and the sunflower meadow."

I must have sounded like a crazy woman. Those letters were intended for Sarah, his wife, not me.

Marco reached over and grabbed my hand.

"Sarge told me all about you. He said you're a great woman. He told me all about the dates."

"I'm sorry Marco... I couldn't resist. Your letters kinda' helped me through a tough time." I closed my eyes. I felt so embarrassed and ashamed. *What an idiot!*

"Oh don't be sorry. I've never told anyone about my mom and the meadow. I'm glad someone was able to read them, apparently Sarah was too busy, if you found them."

Marco walked over to my side of the table and gave me a big hug

"Nia, I'm so sorry I got you involved in this."

Oh God, his body felt sooo good against mine! Nia, stop! Your supposed to be letting Marco go. My thoughts were conflicting each other. I was lying to myself, denying what I truly felt inside. I was in love with him. I loved every little thing about him.

I closed my eyes and kissed Marco's neck. A part of me wanted to take it back, the other part of me wanted him to return my kiss. I could feel Marco's body tense up as my lips left his body.

"Nia, I can't." Marco said as he released himself from my embrace.

"Oh God, I'm soooo sorry. I shouldn't have."

What the hell was I thinking? I wanted to curl up in a ball and fade away. *I just kissed a married man! Marco must hate me!*

Marco rubbed my arm and looked me in the eyes.

"It's not that I don't want to. Nia, I can't. I made a vow to Sarah." Even though his wife was an unappreciative cheating skank, I respected his devotion to her. I think his devotion made my heart swoon even more.

"Nia, you feel ice cold." Marco said while rubbing his hands over my goose bump riddled arms.

"Here, I have something for you." Marco ran over to the closet and pulled out a blanket. He put it over my shoulders and invited me into the living room to sit in front of the fireplace. Marco sat behind me and wrapped his arms around me to keep me warm.

I got so lost in the night. Maybe it was the pearl moon casting it's light through the window or the warm flames of the fireplace or Marco's arms around my body or his breath on my neck. I'm not going to lie. I freaking lost it. I let it all go. I poured my heart out to him. I told him how much I loved him and how his letters were unbelievably romantic. Marco didn't say a word. He simply rubbed my shoulders and listened.

In my heart of hearts, I know we were meant to be. Maybe not at this time, maybe in another universe? I don't know. I just know I love him.

"Nia, I've never met anyone like you. From the first time I saw you, there was something. I don't know what it is. It feels like I have known you forever. I can remember waking up in my mother's meadow and there you were, that beautiful face, my angel. You were smiling. Oh, God that smile, your eyes."

I looked up at Marco and he looked down at me. Our eyes met. Marco smiled. My heart melted and our lips found each other. I could feel my heart spark. It was bliss. I felt an explosion of emotions as I lost my self in his kiss. Afterwards, I placed my head on his chest. Marco held me tight. I fell asleep to the rhythmic beat of his heart. It was our love song, a lovers lullaby. A love that felt so right even though it was not meant to be.

CHAPTER 17: SHATTERED GLASS

The next morning I awoke in Marco's arms. We were snuggled up on the floor in front of the fireplace. Oh, it felt so good! This was the first night of good sleep, I had in a long time. I guess lying on a shag rug in front of a roaring fireplace with your dream lover, will do that to you. If I could, I would stay in the cabin with Marco forever. Him and I excluded from the rest of the world. Two outlaws living off the land.

As good as it sounded, I know the rest of my world was waiting to hear from me. Terence was probably at home worried about me. The last time he saw me was through my father's car window as we drove off in search of Abony. I'm sure the news of Abony, Swag and my father were all over the news. I wish I could have broken the news to my mother first, unfortunately she would find out the horrible news with the rest of the world.

I wiggled out of Marco's warm embrace and walked into the bedroom and grabbed the phone. *Shit! I forgot to turn it off!* I logged into scandal.com to see how the video had spread. To my surprise, the video had over two hundred million views! It was all over social media now. It was the top news story on every website. We weren't out of the woods yet, but I took peace in knowing the Vista's were fully exposed.

Once the news hit, I could imagine Bo and Katy calling a press conference at their home in Buckhead. I could see them sitting on their living room sofa trying to explain their actions to the millions of people around the world watching at home. It would only be a matter of time before Homeland Security came knocking on the Vista's door, wanting to know why they were in bed with the world's most dangerous terrorist. The first question they would ask? Where is Michael Asir Jacques hiding out in Khaberistan? This year alone, Homeland Security has spent millions of dollars and countless hours searching for Michael Asir Jacques and all this time, the world's biggest company had Jacques on speed dial.

Payback is a mother fucker, Katy! Checkmate!

I powered down the phone and prayed to God it wasn't traced. I walked back into the living room and spotted Marco standing by the living room window.

"Is everything OK?" I asked. Marco turned around quickly. My voice had startled him.

"Everything's fine. Something just doesn't feel right. We are going to have to leave this cabin."

"So, what are we going to do? Where will we go?" I asked Marco. "I'm going to have to find a way to sneak into Mexico."

"Don't you mean, WE are going to have to sneak into Mexico?" "Nia, they are only looking for me. The video is live now, so you will be safe. Please, go back to your normal life. Get married, have children. Live your life without me. I'm no good for you."

"Marco, I can't. You're in this mess because of me!"

Out the corner of my eye I could see what looked like a shadow or a silhouette of a person in the brush outside of the window Marco was standing in front of. It looked like one of the cops from last night!

"MARCO! Get DOW….."

Before I could finish my sentence a bullet came crashing through the window, shattering the glass. Marco's eyes opened wide and his body jolted as the bullet pierced right through his right shoulder. Marco dropped to his knees and yelled: "NIA, GET DOWN!" Before I knew it, the front door was knocked off of its hinges. It was the burly officer and his female partner. They found us and had busted through the front door of the cabin. With all the power he could muster, Marco jumped to his feet and tried to stop the officers from entering. The female officer drew her gun and pointed it at Marco.

"Thought you lost us, didn't you! You uploaded that fucking video didn't you!" She said as she fired her gun into Marco's chest.

"MARCO NOOOOOO!!!" I yelled.

Marco gasped for breath as his body rocked backwards. Marco wobbled around before turning to face me. "NIA RUN!"

Marco knew they were not here to arrest us. These officers were given orders to kill us. I could see the terror in Marco's eyes as tears flowed down his face. Bloody and bruised, Marco jumped on the two officers and placed them in a bear hug.

"Marco, are you o.k? I said while approaching the struggle.

"NIA, I can't hold them for long, RUN!!" Marco was right, once the cops where free, they were going to kill me. I fought my emotions and did what I was told. I ran into the back bedroom and went right for the window. The window stuck a little bit but I managed to get free. I heard another loud gunshot and then a large thud. I turned around to get a look before jumping out of the window. Marco lay flat on his back on the ground while the two officers stood above him. *I'm sorry, Marco!* I thought as I dove out of the open window. My feet hit the ground and I ran as fast as I could through the woods that surrounded the old cabin. I was numb.

Marco sacrificed himself so that I could get away. "I love you, Marco" I whispered into the brisk morning air. I ran deep into the woods, never looking back. I prayed Marco was OK.

CHAPTER 18: HOLY MATRIMONY

Today is the big day. I have been waiting for this day for as long as I can remember. It's my special day. It's the day I become Ms. Deveraux. So why am I sad? Why does my heart hurt? Could it be the fact that Abony is gone? Or is it the fact that it's been six months, two hours and thirty six minutes since I saw Marco's lifeless body lying on the cabin floor? My fantasy man, my ghost, the man who I once thought was dead.... is now dead again. At least that's what the news reports say. In my heart of hearts I know it can't be true. Marco has to be alive. A love story is not supposed to end this way.

Right now, I'm kneeling over the toilet in Reverend Gerald Jones bathroom in his personal office at the New Visions First Baptist church. I've been throwing up all day. I can't seem to keep anything down. I have a church full of people out there waiting for me and here I am barfing my guts out.

Despite all of this, life is good. Life is safe again. I don't have to worry about the freckled killer or the Vista's anymore. Katy was arrested and charged with treason and conspiracy to commit terrorism. And Bo, poor Bo, he didn't make it to trial. He was found dead, face down in the bathtub of the Vista's Atlanta home of an apparent opioid overdose. The police report says it was an accident, but knowing what I know, Katy was behind Bo's death. *I hope she rots in prison!*

"Nia, are you ok? Are you coming out?" My mother said from outside of the bathroom. Off in the distance, I could hear the organ in the chapel getting ready to play "Here comes the bride."

That's for me. My cue to walk into the church and take my proper place next to Terence at the alter in front of Reverend Jones and my family and friends. I love Terence and I know he loves me, but part of my heart is elsewhere. Oh, who am I fooling? All of my heart is elsewhere. It's in the grave with the man I love.

"Nia!" My mother called from outside the bathroom door. I stood up and straightened my wedding gown. I looked at myself in the mirror. I had been through a lot, but I still look beautiful. I'm still standing, despite it all. I rubbed my finger across the scar on my chest. What once held the world's biggest secret was now replaced by a butterfly shaped scar. A vivid reminder of how I got here. A symbol of my journey.

I wiped my mouth and opened the bathroom door. My mother stood in front of me in her yellow dress and matching yellow hat. She looked beautiful, like an angel sent from God to help mold me into the woman I am today. For the first time in a long time, mom was smiling. She hasn't really smiled since Abony's death. Today she is happy. You should have seen her face when I asked her to help me prepare our wedding ceremony. The wedding seemed to give her new life, a reason to live again. I think that's why I agreed to marry Terence. It brought some balance to an unbalanced time in my life. My mom and I decided to dedicate the ceremony to the memory of Abony. Even though she couldn't be here physically, I know she is here in spirit.

I made a promise this day that I would do everything in my power to find Andy and raise him as my own. *He will get the life he deserves, Abony. I promise.* Speaking of Andy, that piece of crap Swag was telling the truth. Reverend Sycamore does have my nephew. The reverend used his connections to get full custody of Andy. He claims he has no idea what happened to Abony, but my father and I know the truth. He killed her to get to my nephew. I bet he is going to find a way to exploit Andy's gift. Reverend Sycamore only cares about three things: money, publicity and power. And he will do anything he can, to get it. He has Andy locked up on his compound and he's telling the rest of the world and his naive wife that Andy is his godson. I'm no fool. I know Andy is his child. He may think he got away with it but I will make him pay for what he did to my sister. Karma is a bitch! I will die before I let him keep Andy.

"Are you ok, baby? You look sick." My mother said as she removed her handkerchief from her purse and wiped my brow.

"I'm a little nauseous. It must be my nerves."

"Did you throw-up, baby?"

"Yeah. I can't seem to stomach anything lately. Even the smell of some foods, make me feel sick."

My mother smiled and put her hand on my stomach.

"I dreamed of fish last night."

I sighed and closed my eyes. Someone dreaming of fish, means only one thing in our family. Someone is pregnant. It was an old wives tale but it always turned out to be true. I'm not pregnant, it's my heart hurting.

My mother grabbed my hand and walked me to the lobby of the church. Waiting for me at the church doors was my father. He sat slumped over in his wheelchair, waiting to give his daughter's hand away in marriage. The doctors say he's lucky to be alive. The shooting left my poor father paralyzed from the waist down. One of the bullets he took for me is embedded in his spine. He looks frail and old now. His once jet black hair and beard is now as white as snow. He looks handsome, though. The dark tuxedo made him look like some old sophisticated Mafia Don who put his first tux on to celebrate his daughter's wedding.

"You look... beautiful.. Nia!" My father struggled to say through the respirator attached to his nostrils.

"Thank you, Dad." I replied with a smile.

"You get.... your beauty... from the most.... beautiful... woman in the world." My father said as he glanced down the aisle at my mother.

"You know you don't have to do this right? Cliff can walk me down the aisle." I said.

"It is... my honor, sweetheart. I wouldn't...miss this... for anything... in the world! Nia...I'm proud...of you!" My father struggled to speak.

"Well, what are we waiting for? Let's get this over with!" I said while grabbing a hold of my father's arm. I gave the ushers a smile and a nod, signaling them to open the church doors. The entire church stood as we approached the front of the aisle. Terence stood at the altar, looking just as handsome as can be. His big dimpled smile and that black tux made me forget about all of my troubles.

"He's... a ...good man, Nia. He's going... to make a great.. husband." My father said.

My brother Cliff stood by Terence's side as his best man and Harley was on the other side of them. She was the most beautiful maid of honor I have ever seen in my life. Next to her was a pedestal holding a large picture of Abony flanked by a beautiful flower arrangement. I took a deep breath and held on to my father's arm as we strolled down the aisle. Tears flowed down my cheeks as we walked past all of my family and friends. Everything was perfect. I took my place next to Terence. Reverend Jones stood in front of us and began the ceremony. Terence had the crowd wooing when recited his vow's to me.

"Nia, I have waited for this moment all of my life. You are my rock, my queen. I am everything with you and nothing without you. I vow to you today that I will love you forever. I devote my life to making you happy. I devote my life to making you smile. To my last dying breath, I will give you everything you deserve. I thought I lost you once. I will never lose you again. I love you, Nia"

Awwww…. Terence made my heart melt and my legs wobble. We were doing it. We were getting married. Reverend Jones gave me the nod. It was now my turn to say my vows. I had practiced them all week. I was ready. I looked deep into Terence's eyes. I was just about to speak when Harley leaned in behind me and whispered in my ear.

"Nia, look at the last pew in the back of the church."

What in the world is she talking about? I am about to recite my vows! I don't have time to look at the last pew! I humored Abony and tilted my head slightly, glancing at the last pew out of the corner of my eye.

WHAT???!!!!

There was a clean shaven man dressed in a rusty leather jacket and big dark sunglasses sitting in the back of the church. He lowered his sunglasses ever so slightly and smiled. IT WAS FREAKING MARCO!!!!

The reverend tapped me on the shoulder bringing me back to attention. My mind went blank and my stomach filled with butterflies as I struggled to remember the vows I had spent all week trying to memorize. *Get it together, Nia!* After a few nerve racking moments, my vows came back to me.

"Marco, I promise to give you my heart. We were destined to be…."
Terence eyes opened wide. He looked shocked.

MARCO! Oh shit! Did I just call Terence, MARCO??
Terence leaned in and whispered "Did you just say Marco?" I struggled
with my words as I tried to start my vows over. I could hear the wedding
guests in the church whispering amongst themselves.

"Oh no she didn't?"

"Did she just called him another man's name?"

"Woooh… she called him Marco!" They whispered.

Keep going, Nia…keep going. You can do this!

I gathered my composure and swallowed my pride as the words of my
vows oozed from my lips. I told <u>TERENCE</u> I wanted to marry him after
the first day we met. I thanked him for being there for me and I told him I
loved him. I'm not going to lie, my eyes kept drifting back to Marco in the
back pew. *Why was he here?*
After my vows, the Reverend continued the ceremony.

"If anyone can show just cause or have an objection to this holy
matrimony. Let them speak now or forever hold their peace." The
Reverend professed to the crowd. He was about to continue the ceremony
when Marco stood up in the back pew.

"I OBJECT!" Marco said from the back of the church. His words
vibrated through the crowd and hung in the air like a sour music note.
Everyone in the church turned and looked in his direction.

"Well, I don't object. I have a confession I want to make to the bride,
before she devotes her life to this man."

Oh God Marco, what are you doing!!? Marco removed his sunglasses and placed his hand over his heart.

"Nia, before you get married I want the world to know that you are a great woman. Terence, congratulations, you are lucky man. You are marrying the most beautiful woman in the world. Before I go back in to hiding, forever. Nia, I want to let you know that I am in love with you!" The entire wedding party gasped and my mother almost fainted in the front pew.

"Why in the world would you interrupt this ceremony, son?" The reverend said angrily.

"I'm sorry Rev. I'm in love with Nia and I don't care who knows! Nia, I can't stop thinking about you!"

"USHERS, PLEASE GET HIM OUT OF HERE!" Reverend Jones commanded. The two young ushers at the door, who just so happened to be Terence's cousins, rushed Marco. They grabbed a hold of his arms and started pulling him out of the church. That didn't stop Marco from professing his love as they dragged him through the church doors.

Before I realized what I was doing, I was halfway down the aisle, chasing after the man I love. Terence grabbed a hold of my arm.

"Nia, what are you doing? You can't leave me like this!

"Terence, I'm sorry." Is all I could say.

"Nia, don't!"

My heart took over for my feet and I continued my run down the aisle. Away from Terence and away from my commitment to be his wife. I could hear the crowd gasp as I ran down the aisle. I slammed the doors open. Marco was getting into a dark colored SUV.

Thank God he's not gone!

"MAAARCO!" I yelled at the top of my lungs. Marco froze in his tracks and turned his head in my direction. The look of confusion on his face slowly morphed into a smile.

"NIA, GO BACK!" Marco yelled back, right before getting into the car. "I LOVE YOU TOO, MARCO!" I yelled back. I kicked off my heels, hiked up my dress and bolted down the front steps of the church. I was not going to lose this man again! I ran over to the passenger side of the SUV, opened the door and hopped in.

"Nia, what are you doing? Go back to the church!"

"Marco, I thought they killed you!" My lipped quivered.

"I did too! All I remember is the cops breaking into the cabin and then the next thing I remember is waking up in a hospital in Mexico a few days later. All bandaged up."

"I'm so glad you're alive!" I pressed my head up against his chest. I could feel the rhythm of his heartbeat against my cheek, like that night in the cabin.

"Nia, I'm a freaking outlaw. I'm no good for you! They think I killed Sarah's lover. I have to go back to Mexico."

"So you knew about Sarah and her trainer?"

"Well, I always suspected her. I'm no fool. I loved her. Hell, I still have love for her. But, I didn't kill Todd. It had to be the Vista's trying to frame me." It all made sense. I knew Marco was innocent but that doesn't help Marco. The Vista's made him a wanted man.

Off in the distance, outside of the car, I could hear someone yell my name. "NIIIIAAAAA!" It was Terence. He was standing at the entrance of the church.

"Oh God Marco, I can't do it. Pull off!"

"Are you sure?" Marco replied.

"Yes, I am sure. Please go!"

"Your wish is my command." Marco started the car and put his feet on the gas. *I can't believe I'm doing this!*

Terence looked frantic as he bolted down the stairs of the church and out to the churches parking lot. Terence jumped in front of the car.

THUUUUMP! Is all I heard as Terence's body smacked off of Marco's car. Marco slammed his foot on the brake and the car came to a grinding halt. Terrence's body hit the car hard and like a rag doll, he rolled hard off of the front of the hood and onto the ground.

"TERENCE!!!" I yelled as I sat up in my seat, afraid to see the damage the car did to my fiancé. I have to be the only bride in history to run over her groom on their wedding day. The entire wedding party and all the guests were outside now. They looked on in horror as Terence struggled to get back to his feet. *Thank God, he's alive!* Terence crawled onto the hood of the car. He was determined not to let me go.

"Nia, please don't go!" Terence said through the windshield of the car right before passing out and rolling off and on to the ground, again. My mother and brother rushed over and helped Terence back up to his feet.

"Damn, Nia. I think this man loves you! My heart is telling me to put the car in drive and take you away with me, but my mind says different. This life is not for you, Nia. Get out and marry that man. He loves you. He will give you a better life than I can ever give you. Plus I really don't think he is going to take no for an answer." Marco joked.

Marco rubbed my shoulder and gave me a kiss on the forehead. "I love you, now and forever, Nia. Maybe we can do this in another life." Marco said with a smile. As much as I hate to admit it, Marco was right. I had to let him go. This whole situation was not good for me. I gave Marco a giant hug and then I kissed his cheek. I stared in his eyes for a few moments… "Marco, I will miss you!"

I was greeted with a large cheer when I got out of the car. *What a freaking wedding day!* Terence hobbled over to me. His brand new tux was ripped to shreds. *We hit him good.* Poor Terence. He was willing to jump in front of a car for me.

"Terence are you O.K.?"

"Nia, I'm not going to lose you again!" Terence got down on one knee and held up the most beautiful wedding ring I had ever seen in my life. He was proposing to me for the third time. How could I say no? I looked down at his watery eyes and big dimpled smile.

"Nia, I love you. Will you marry me?" I looked over at Marco. He gave me a wink and a smile right before he put the car in drive. *In my life one minute and out of my life in another.* I cherished the time I had with him. I will always love him.

"Yes, I will marry you Terence!" The crowd cheered as I extended my hand. Terence placed the ring on my finger.

"Hold on, let me make this official, while I have a chance!" Reverend Jones said as he stepped out from the crowd and stood in front of Terence and I.

"Terence, do you take Nia, to be your lawfully wedded wife?"

"I so do!" Terence professed.

Nia, do you take Terence to be your lawfully wedded husband?" All eyes were on me. This was my moment.

"Yes, I do." I replied.

"Thank you Lord! By the power vested in me in the state of Georgia, I now pronounce you husband and wife! You may kiss the bride!" Terence and I shared our first married kiss right there in the parking lot of New Visions First Baptist church. We were finally married.

I was now Nia Wright Deveroux.

EPILOGUE: FAIRY TALE ENDING?

What a crazy year it's been. My life has changed in ways I could have never imagined. Did I get my fairy tale ending? Did I make the right choice? I guess I will never know. What I do know?... I'm happy. I'm in a good place, right now. Nia, got her groove back!

After the wedding, Terence and I went on a month long honeymoon. We spent days lying on a private beach in Bermuda staring up at the fluffiest clouds I have ever seen in my life. The white sand, the sound of the waves, the seagulls squawking off in the distance, the island drums.... It was paradise! It gave us a chance to reconnect and get to know each other again, which has helped our marriage tremendously.

My mother is doing better, she joined us in Bermuda for a week. It was good for her to get away from the city so she could clear her mind. Now, my father on the other hand, he is still not out of the woods. But he is doing a little better. The doctors say he will probably never walk again, but he is expected to make a full recovery as long as he continues his therapy. I spend every morning with my father making sure he is taking care of himself, going to therapy and taking his medication. He is a stubborn old man, but I keep him on track.

We actually broke ground on the Abony Bella Wright School For Girls, in Decatur Georgia. It will be an all girl's school that will have state of the art computers, science lab, mathematics lab, all the things needed to give these young girls a competitive advantage and a great education.

I even hired a private detective to get information on Reverend Sycamore. The battle to get Andy back is not going to be easy. I am going to have to go through the legal system to get him back. If that doesn't work, I am willing to do whatever it takes, legal or illegal to get my nephew back.

I just finished my late morning jog after a half hour workout with my personal trainer. Can you believe I lost fifteen pounds? I guess working out and cutting out sugar can work miracles on the body. As I approached my driveway I spotted the mailman and his little mail truck parked near my mailbox.

"Ed, you're early today." I said to my mailman. I tried not to get too close. I was covered in sweat from my jog. No need for him to smell my funk.

"That's right Ms. Deveroux, we are expecting some heavy thunderstorms today, so I figured I would get an early start. Ed reached in his bag and pulled out a few pieces of mail and a small box.

"Here you go, Ms. Deveroux. You have a good day!"

"Thank you Ed. Make sure you say hello to Clara for me!"
I walked back into the house, via the garage and plopped all the mail on the island in the kitchen. I had no big interest in opening them right now. It was either a bill or a bunch of junk mail, anyway. I walked over to the fridge and grabbed a bottle of water. I gulped it down like a beast. I swear drinking water now, makes my skin look unbelievable. As I gulped, I noticed the handwriting on the small box. *It can't be!* I've see that handwriting before. *Is that Marco's handwriting?* I almost spit my water out all over the kitchen counter! I rushed over to the box and picked it up. A faint smell of Marco's cologne was oozing from the box. My heart began to race. *No way!*

I closed my eyes and put the box under my nose. I inhaled and took in all of its essence. The smell brought me right back to Marco and our first date. I ran to the living room and plopped down on the couch. Thank goodness, Terence is in Ghana for the next three weeks training some young surgeons. If he saw this box, he would flip.

I ripped open the box. There were two letters and a can of beefaroni inside. *Marco is nuts!* I laughed to myself. The first letter had "To my hero, Nia. Loving you while I'm gone" written on the outside of the letter. My heart skipped several beats as I unfolded the letter and began to read.

Dear Nia,

I thought living without you would be easy. I can't lie. I feel incomplete without you. I need you by my side even though I know I can't have you here with me. I made a promise that I would not interfere with your life. Nia, baby… I can't let you go. I know I can't be their physically but we can still have each other in our minds. In this box is another letter, a date letter. I know you know what to do with it. It's up to you. I will totally understand if you throw this letter in the ocean and never read it again. In either case, know that I will always love you.

Love, Marco

I went right to the second letter. There was no need to wait! On the outside of the letter it read:

Loving you while I'm gone- First date

Nia,

If you have come this far, then you have agreed to go on this special date with me. I'm glad we can be together, even if it is only in our minds. I've planned something very special for our first official date. You know what to do, call 413-237-6150, if you dare!

Love Marco

Without a second thought, I grabbed my phone and dialed the number in Marco's letter. The phone rang several times. In my heart of hearts I hoped I would hear Sarge's voice on the other end. It wasn't Sarge who answered. It was a woman with a sweet voice and a strong Chinese accent.

"Hello, how may I help you?" The woman answered.

"Hi… this is Nia…I am calling about a letter I received." I replied nervously.

"Oh Nia, I am glad to hear from you! We have been waiting for your call. Are you ready for a wonderful time?

"Yes I am! I think."

"Great! The car will be by your house in an hour to pick you up and take you to the airport."

"The airport? Did you just say airport? Can I ask you where you are taking me?"

'Sorry madam, it is supposed to be a surprise, but I can tell you that the Xiagei Hot Springs in Shangri-La China are beautiful this time of year."

"Did you just say China!?"

"Yes, ma'am, Xiagei Hot Springs are in China. Please make sure you have your passport and don't bother with luggage. We have that taken care of for you. See you in an hour!" The lady responded.

Marco, Marco, Marco…. What are you up to?

I ran to the bedroom and grabbed my passport from my suitcase. *Nia, what are you doing? What if Terence finds out? Well, I should only be gone for a few days. He will never know. Plus, it's not like I'm actually going on a real date.* That's what I told myself. I had to go with my heart despite my gut instinct. I don't know what Marco has planned but I was ready for our next adventure. *Here we go again.*